# Courtwright pointed a finger at Butler. "I want him."

"What can I do for you, Sheriff?"

"You can give me your gun and come with me," Sheriff Courtwright said. "You're under arrest."

"For what?"

"Suspicion of murder."

"No."

Sheriff Courtwright looked confused, then trapped. He turned to his deputies. "Take him, boys."

Butler and Short both drew their guns.

"Are you crazy?" Courtwright asked. "Drawing your guns on the law?"

"Right now, we don't recognize your authority," Short said.

Courtwright turned to his deputies. "I said, take 'em in."

The two deputies gave him a look that said, 'Why don't you take them yourself?'

"Damnit!" Courtwright said. "I'll have your badges."

The deputies exchanged looks, then unpinned their badges. "You can have 'em," one of the men said. And they handed their tin to the sheriff.

## By Robert J. Randisi

### THE GAMBLERS

*Butler's Wager*
*Denver Draw*
*Texas Bluff*

### THE SONS OF DANIEL SHAYE

*Leaving Epitaph*
*Vengeance Creek*
*Pearl River Junction*

# ROBERT J. RANDISI

## THE GAMBLERS
# TEXAS BLUFF

# HARPER

*An Imprint of HarperCollinsPublishers*

This is a work of fiction. Names, characters, places, and incidents are products of the author's imagination or are used fictitiously and are not to be construed as real. Any resemblance to actual events, locales, organizations, or persons, living or dead, is entirely coincidental.

**HARPER**

*An Imprint of* HarperCollins*Publishers*
10 East 53rd Street
New York, New York 10022-5299

Copyright © 2008 by Robert J. Randisi
ISBN: 978-0-06-089019-3

First Harper paperback printing: February 2008

HarperCollins® and Harper® are registered trademarks of Harper-Collins Publishers.

Printed in the United States of America

Visit Harper paperbacks on the World Wide Web at
www.harpercollins.com

10   9   8   7   6   5   4   3

# THE GAMBLERS
# TEXAS BLUFF

# CHAPTER 1

————◆————

Butler had decided to try to hit every major gambling hall in Texas before he continued on his way to California. What he didn't expect was that it would take him a year.

Upon leaving Colorado after an adventure in Denver with Bat Masterson and Doc Holliday he drifted for a while, stopping here and there along the way when he found a likely poker game. He worked his way down toward Texas, and when he heard about a saloon or a gambling hall that sounded interesting, that's where he went.

Once he got to Texas he found himself playing poker in Jack Harris's Saloon and Vaudeville Theater in San Antonio. This was after Harris had been killed by Ben Thompson, who went on trial for murder. Butler knew Thompson, but did not get to see him during that time.

Then he played for a while at the Iron Front in Austin, which was actually owned by Ben Thompson. But Thompson was still having trouble over the Harris thing, so once again Butler did not get to see him.

In El Paso he won quite a bit of money in Ben Dowell's Saloon. This was after Dowell had died on his ranch, just outside of town.

The reason Butler remembered these three stopovers more than others was that, in addition to doing well in all three saloons, there was an attempt on his life in all three places. Obviously, the price put on his head by someone back East was still enforced. He'd thwarted dozens of attempts on his life over the years, and he remembered every one of them.

Approximately one year after the events in Denver, Butler rode into Fort Worth, Texas. He checked into a hotel down the street from the White Elephant Saloon, which was his ultimate goal. This would be his last Texas stop before he finally continued on his way to California.

He chose the hotel because it was large, had its own livery stable and a doorman in front. In other words, it reeked of luxury. He'd been doing so well at the tables lately that he decided to treat himself.

Butler was no stranger to luxury. Growing up in the East, his family had been well off. Later, when he was exiled to the West and started to make his living playing poker, he would treat himself whenever he was flush. And the better he became, the more often he was flush.

His room was a two-room suite. The bedroom had a large bed with a thick mattress, and not only a dresser for his clothes but a wardrobe to hang his suits in.

The outer room was set up like a living room or sitting room, complete with plush armchair and sofa and a small sidebar with decanters for various types of liquor. The furnishings were maroon and gold, very rich feeling. He approved of his new digs, which was important, because he planned to be there for a while. He'd learned the word *digs* from a Brit he played poker against in Chicago. He liked it, but never said it out loud to anyone.

After a bath he put on a clean black suit, a boiled white shirt, and a black string tie. He did not wear jewelry, probably never would, no matter how much money he had. He looked at gamblers who wore diamond cuff links and stickpins and thought they were too flashy, like tinhorns. The last thing he put on was his flat-crowned black hat with a silver band and a three-and-a-half-inch brim.

He was ready to check out the White Elephant Saloon.

Luke Short was the new one-third owner of the White Elephant. His partner, Bill Ward, had been determined to change the image of the White Elephant, to hopefully bring in some big-name gamblers. For that he needed a partner who knew some big-name gamblers. When he met Luke Short he was sure he'd found his man.

Short's first move was to change the physical image of the saloon. He had the public area decorated with fancy rosewood and mahogany fixtures that he had brought in from back East. He also brought in something that became known as the "Luke Short Bar." It was mahogany, made in three pieces, and covered most of one wall of the saloon. He added onyx and crystal to the décor, immediately giving the place a touch of class. The last thing he did was to introduce the game of keno to Fort

Worth, which caught fire and added substantially to the saloon's profit margin.

"Little Luke" had placed his personal stamp on the White Elephant and—just as Bill Ward had hoped—the big-name gamblers began to come.

# CHAPTER 2

Butler was impressed with the White Elephant Saloon as soon as he entered. It was easily the largest gaming hall he'd ever been in, and it apparently had some other, private, rooms where—more than likely—its high-stakes games took place.

Butler had heard that famed gambler Luke Short was now part owner of the White Elephant. He knew that Short was good friends with both Bat Masterson and Wyatt Earp, two legendary lawmen and gamblers who had become his friends over the past couple of years. Both of those men admitted that Luke Short was probably a better man with a deck of cards than either of them was. Butler was looking forward to meeting the man he'd heard so much about.

He approached the vast bar and easily found a place for himself, even though the saloon was buzzing with activity.

He ordered a beer, and when it came the mug was frosty, almost too cold to pick up.

"Is this place always this busy?" he asked the bartender.

"You ain't never been in here before, have you?" the man asked.

"No," Butler said. "I just got to town."

"The answer is yes," the bartender said. "It is always this busy in here."

"I heard you have private rooms."

"We've got lots of rooms," the man said. "The owners live upstairs, and Mr. Short has a special room for high-stakes poker games."

"Ah," Ty Butler said, "that's the one I'm interested in."

"I thought you had the look of a gambler when you walked in," the bartender said, "but people only get to play in that game by invitation."

"And how do I get invited?"

"Do you know Mr. Short?"

"No, but—"

"What's your name?"

"Butler."

The man shook his head.

"I don't know the name" he said, "so you ain't famous."

"No," Butler agreed, "I'm not famous."

"Then you ain't gettin' invited," the man said. "Not unless you do something to get yerself noticed by Mr. Short himself."

"I might just have something," Butler said.

"Well, you better trot it on out, then," the bartender said. "Gotta go. Duty calls."

The bar was so long there were two bartenders serving drinks.

"'Scuse me," the man next to him said.

Butler turned to look at him. He was well dressed—although not as well dressed as Butler—and had the look of a man fresh from a bath and shave. He smelled of bay rum and his mustache was carefully curled on the ends.

"I couldn't help hearin' your conversation," the man said. "I've been tryin' to get into one of Luke Short's private games for weeks."

"Pretty tough to do, huh?" Butler asked. "The bartender seems to think I'd need to know somebody."

"I know Short's partner, Bill Ward," the man said, "and I still can't get invited."

"Wow," Butler said, "that does sound tough."

The man put his hand out and said, "Al Newman. I heard you say you just got to Fort Worth. I live here. Welcome."

"Ty Butler," Butler said, shaking the man's hand.

"I come here every night, have a beer, gamble upstairs, and hope I'll do something that will attract Luke Short's attention."

"Well," Butler said, "you could shoot somebody."

"I don't want that much attention."

"Doesn't look like there's much going on here in the way of gambling," Butler said. "Upstairs, you say?"

"That's where the real casino is," Newman said. "You go up this long stairway, passing the losers who are comin' down."

"Well," Butler said, "that sounds like the place I should be."

"Finish up your beer, my new friend, and I'll show you how to get up there."

Butler was really in no hurry to finish the beer. It was

cold, and the taste was excellent. Newman had a similar brew in front of him. So they finished up together while Newman told Butler he had a business in town.

"I'm a lawyer," he said.

"Criminal lawyer?"

"As a matter of fact, yes," Newman said.

"Since you say you're a friend of Luke's partner, I'm going to guess that you're a fairly prominent lawyer."

"I'd say you were right," Newman said. "Fact is I ran for district attorney one year. Didn't win, but yeah, I guess I'm fairly well known."

"And even that can't get you into one of the private games?" Butler asked.

"Luke Short is impressed with what people can do at a poker table, not what they do in their everyday lives."

"Well," Butler said, "I guess I'm ready to go up and have a look at where all the action takes place."

They both drained their mugs and Newman said, "Follow me."

# CHAPTER 3

"Why not Al Newman?" Bill Ward asked Luke Short. "You say you're lookin' for another man?"

"I'm not just lookin' for another body, Bill," Short said. "I'm lookin' for a poker player."

"Well, there are plenty of them downstairs, too," Ward said. "Pick one."

"Do you know why all these men want to get into the private games, Bill?"

"I'm sure you're going to tell me."

"Because they are private," Short said. "If anybody could sit in, these men would be lookin' elsewhere."

"Look, Bill," he continued, "when I bought in we agreed I'd handle the gambling—especially the big games with the big names, right?"

"That's what we said, Luke."

They were in the office that was generally considered to belong to Bill Ward. Since it was Short who bought into Ward's property, he insisted Ward keep it. Now he approached Ward, who was seated behind the desk, and put his hand on the man's shoulder.

"So why don't you stop tryin' to get me to let your friends in to play?"

Ward threw up his hands and said, "Okay, okay, I'm done."

"I'm gonna go out and see how we're doin' tonight," Luke said.

"I'll go downstairs and say hello to some friends," Ward said.

He stood up and they both left the office together. They were standing in a hall that would lead them each to where they wanted to go. This was another of Luke Short's improvements. He had the hall built, and they could get downstairs or upstairs from there.

"Have a good night," Ward said to Short.

"Let's just have a productive night," Short said. "That's what counts."

Ward shook his head as Luke Short walked down to the other end of the hall. Once again he silently congratulated himself for having chosen the right partner . . . this time around. Short was his third partner in as many years, but Bill Ward felt that this time he'd finally gotten it right. He turned and walked to the other end of the hall.

Butler was impressed with the setup.

As Newman had predicted, they walked up the long enclosed stairwell and had to step aside to let some grim-looking men down.

"Losers," Newman said to Butler.

"Is there another stairway for the winners?" Butler asked.

"Who are you kiddin'?" Newman said. "Nobody leaves here a winner."

"Then why do they come?" Butler was a good card player. At this point in his life he hardly considered it gambling. He usually won. If he never won another game, he wondered how long he would go on playing?

"They can't not come," Newman said. "They each have their game, and they have to come and play it. It's not like they have a choice."

Butler had known compulsive gamblers, but he did not understand the malady.

They continued up the stairs and when Butler came out into the casino, he was impressed. There were some poker games being played downstairs, and the faro game, but this . . . everywhere he looked a game was going on, and the room seemed to have every game imaginable. He saw blackjack, poker, faro, red dog, roulette, craps, and a couple of tables of games he did not recognize.

"What's your game?" Newman asked.

"Poker."

"No," the lawyer said, "I mean other than poker."

"I usually just play poker, Al."

"Well then, that explains why you're so much better dressed than I am," Newman said. "If I can't get into a poker game I'll play almost anything else. I prefer blackjack, but there are times I can't resist the lure of the roulette wheel, or the dice."

Yes, Butler said to himself, that is why I'm better dressed than you are.

"Well," Butler said, "you go ahead and find a game.

I'll walk around and take a look. I have been known to play a few hands of blackjack, though not often. There are just too many times the dealer has twenty-one to your twenty for my taste."

"I know what you mean," Newman said.

"Good luck," Butler said.

"Thanks. If I catch up to you later I'll buy you a drink—or, if I'm broke, you can buy me one."

"You're on," Butler said.

He had a feeling he knew who was going to be doing the buying.

# CHAPTER 4

Butler found a smaller bar upstairs, got himself another cold beer to carry around as he looked the place over. Every table was filled to capacity, but there always seemed to be room for one more, especially at the roulette wheels and the crap tables. All the seats were filled at the blackjack and faro tables. The only place he could have gambled with cards seemed to be the red dog table, but he wasn't interested.

There were women working the floor, carrying drinks and carrying on with the men, distracting them from their gambling any way they could. It was a good ploy for the house, getting the players liquored up, or just getting them thinking about something else—like what was going on in their pants.

Butler was a serious poker player. He didn't drink to excess at the table, and if a woman wanted his attention she was going to have to wait until he was finished with his business.

He was nursing the beer he had now because he'd had one downstairs already. If he ended up in a poker game tonight, his head had to be clear.

He kept his eyes open for Luke Short. Bat Masterson had described Short as a natty little dresser, prone to wearing a silk top hat and carrying a walking stick. He also told Butler that "Little Luke" was a hell of a man to have behind you in a fight. He said a lot of men had been fooled by Short's size.

Armed with this description, Butler was able to spot Luke Short with no problem. Sporting both the silk hat and cane, the man was working his way through the assemblage of gamblers, slapping some on the back, exchanging waves with others. He seemed to be very popular with the gamblers.

Butler wasn't sure how to play this. Should he approach Short and announce their mutual friendship with both Bat Masterson and Wyatt Earp? Or just wait and see if he could impress him, attract Short's attention through his normal play?

Butler decided to take another look at the poker tables. Maybe he'd see somebody he knew, somebody who could simply introduce him to Luke Short. But not only did he not find anyone who would fit that bill, there were no open chairs at the table. He watched for a while, but it soon became clear that there were no professionals in the bunch. He could have waited for an open chair and fleeced some sheep, but there was no challenge in that.

He needed to find a real game. That was what he came to the White Elephant for.

"You don't look happy," someone said.

He turned and found Luke Short standing next to him, looking amused.

"Luke Short," Butler said, surprised.

"You know me?" Short said.

"Just by reputation, and a friend described you to me."

"A friend?"

"Bat Masterson." Hell, why not? It had fallen in his lap.

Now Short looked surprised.

"You know Bat? Where from?"

"Dodge City," Butler said. "I was there with Jim for a little while, and then Bat. Later Trinidad, and then Denver."

"The Doc Holliday thing in Denver?"

"That's right."

Now Short looked delighted.

"You're Butler."

"That's right."

"Tyrone Butler, if I remember correctly."

"Yes."

"Sir, what a pleasure! Why, I must have just missed you in Dodge."

Short stuck out his hand and Butler shook it.

"How long have you been here? Why didn't you look me up?" Short demanded.

"I just arrived today, and I had no idea you'd know who I am," Butler said.

"I have seen Bat since that thing in Denver and he told me all about you. Seems you're the main reason Jim is still alive, and perhaps even Doc Holliday—though barely."

"Bat gives me too much credit."

"Nonsense," Short said. "You are modest. Bat speaks the truth about the men he's met. It's the only reason he admits that Ben Thompson is the best man he's ever seen with a gun." Short made a face. "Believe me, none of us like to admit that."

"This is quite a place," Butler said, to change the subject. "Why did you happen to walk over to me?"

"Well, you were starin' at the poker tables, lookin' so forlorn. I knew it must be because you didn't approve of the talent. That, or you couldn't wait to sit down and take the money."

"There's not enough talent—or money—here to make it worthwhile." Butler hoped he didn't sound too full of himself.

"Well," Luke Short said, taking Butler by the arm and leading him away, "we can fix that."

# CHAPTER 5

———◆———

Butler was surprised at how quickly his fortunes had changed. In truth, it probably would not have happened had Luke Short not been desperately looking for some high-stakes poker players.

Short admitted as much as he walked Butler to one of the private rooms.

"I'm afraid I've been driven to trollin' for poker players," he said. "When I saw your face I knew you were disappointed in what you were seein'."

"Well," Butler replied, "since we're telling the truth, I was trying to figure out how to get invited into one of your games. I'd been told by a bartender downstairs, and one of your customers, that it was almost impossible."

"Which customer?"

"A fella named Newman? Al Newman. Said he was a lawyer who once ran—"

"—for district attorney, yes. My partner, Bill Ward, has been tryin' to get me to let Newman into one of the games."

"Yes, he said he was friends with Ward, and that didn't help."

"Doesn't help, doesn't hurt," Short said. "I'm afraid Mr. Newman is just not up to the caliber of player I'm lookin' for."

"What makes you think I am?"

"Let's just say that Bat gave you his all-around endorsement. Here we are."

Short opened a door and allowed Butler to precede him into the room. Inside he saw one table with five men seated at it. There was one extra, empty chair.

"Usually I fill this game out myself," Short said. "I was close to doing that tonight. In fact, I was close to letting Al Newman in, but now I have you."

Butler almost felt bad, as if he was taking the seat right out from under Al Newman.

Short took Butler up to the table, waited for the hand that was in progress to be completed, and then introduced him.

"Gents, this young feller is Tyrone Butler, a good friend of mine and of Bat Masterson's."

That was one way to get people's attention, and it worked.

"Butler, around the table starting here are Dick Clark, Charlie Coe, Jake Johnson, John Tunney, and that feller there is Jack Archer, otherwise known as—"

"—Three-Eyed Jack," Butler finished.

He circled the table and shook hands with Jack, who he had last seen in Wichita over two years ago. Jack rose and the two pumped hands.

"You two obviously know each other," Short said.

"A coupla years back me and this young feller terrorized the gamblers in Wichita for a time," Jack explained.

"You know," Butler said, "I never did hear your last name back then."

"Don't use it much," Jack said.

"What're you doing here?" Butler asked. "Last I heard you were going to stay in Wichita."

"I did for a while, but then it dried up real bad. I had no choice but to leave. Found my way here a couple of weeks ago, decided to stay."

"He can't leave," Clark said good-naturedly, "he's got all our money."

"Your money, maybe," Coe said.

"Can we get this game back on track?" John Tunney asked. "The only way I'm gonna get my money back is to keep these cards in the air."

"Sorry," Short said, "didn't mean to disrupt the game. I was just bringin' Butler in to fill the last chair."

"Good," Johnson said, "maybe that'll change Jack's luck."

"Buy in's three thousand to start, Butler," Short said.

"Not a problem," Butler said.

"Re-buy as many times as you want, after that," Short said.

"No chips?" Butler asked, seating himself at the table.

"Cash plays," Jack said, reseating himself as well. "I like the sound of paper money."

"Especially other people's, huh, Jack?" Clark asked

Butler knew Dick Clark by reputation. The man had made a fortune in the mining camps of Colorado, and had never dirtied his hands. It had all been done with cards.

He also recognized Charlie Coe's name from the circuit. He'd never played against him, but knew men who had.

He didn't know the others, but he intended to. He'd spend a few hands getting to know them real well before he actually began to get involved in the game.

# CHAPTER 6

———◆———

"Your friend doesn't seem to want to cross swords, Jack," Dick Clark said.

"Don't worry about Butler, Dick," Jack said, with a smile. "He's waitin' for the right moment."

"Seems to me he's just takin' up space," Tunney remarked.

Butler knew this jibe was designed to get him mad so he'd make a mistake, get involved in a hand he wasn't strong in. But Butler always maintained his composure at the poker table. It was one of the reasons he won as often as he did.

As he watched the players he ranked them in his head. Three-Eyed Jack was a good poker player, but he wasn't in the same league with Dick Clark and Charlie Coe. He had taken so much of their money because he was on an incredible hot streak. In fact, since Butler sat down Jack had taken money from Tunney and Johnson, who kept going in with him, but the two professionals, Clark and Coe, had started to stay away from him.

Butler laid back a little longer than he usually did, but poker players who knew what they were doing were harder to read than total amateurs. With an amateur you know almost immediately how often they bluff. In point of fact professionals only bluffed when the size of the pot warranted it. A huge pot was worth trying to steal with a bluff. A small pot was a waste of time.

Jack was not bluffing. He had the cards every time he bet. That's what happened when you were on a hot streak.

The few times that Jack folded, either Coe or Clark would take the ante. The other two men—Johnson and Tunney—were losing heavily.

After almost an hour Butler started to play his game. From that point on, whenever Jack sat a hand out, it was Coe, Clark, or Butler who took the hand.

They played that way for hours, and Butler wondered where Johnson and Tunney got all the money they were losing?

And then it happened.

Three-Eyed Jack cooled off, and tried to bluff.

Jack was the only man Butler had played against before, and he needed only a few hands to remind him how the man played. When his luck cooled, Butler was able to see it before the others.

On the hand where Jack's luck turned, Coe and Clark had already folded, believing that the man once again had the goods.

The other two chased him again, while chasing their hands.

The hand was seven-card stud. Five cards were out when Jack made his big bet.

His bluff.

Jack had a jack, queen, and king of hearts on the

table, and two cards in the hole. But he wasn't high on the table. That honor went to Tunney, who was showing two nines.

"I bet two hundred," Tunney said, ignoring Jack's three to the royal.

Next came Johnson, who had a small pair of fours. He raised, going another two hundred, which led Butler to believe the man either had another pair in the hole, or a third four. He wasn't going to make four of a kind, though, because Coe had folded a four. Butler doubted Johnson remembered that.

It was four hundred to Butler.

"Call," he said.

He had a deuce, a five, and a ten on the table, mismatched.

"You callin' with garbage like that on the table, Butler?" Tunney asked. "You must have some pair in the hole, or just some pair of *cojones*."

"The play is to you, Jack," Charlie Coe said.

"I'm gonna raise four hundred, boys," Jack said with a smile. The smile was not a giveaway—he always smiled when he raised. But he looked at his hole cards. Jack never looked at his hole cards, he always knew what was there. The fact that he looked led Butler to believe he was bluffing, wanted the table to think he either already had the royal, or at least had four to it. The fact was he'd probably take the hand with just a flush. However, Butler had seen four hearts go under when Coe and Clark folded, and both Tunney and Johnson had one on the table. He had one in the hole. That meant that ten hearts were gone, and Jack only had three more in the deck he could catch—unless they were already in his hand.

But Butler didn't think they were.

Tunney—the original bettor—called both raises, and Johnson called Jack's raise.

Butler could have reraised there, but he decided to wait. He just smooth called and waited.

Coe was dealing, so he said, "Pot's right. Comin' out."

He dealt each player their sixth card.

# CHAPTER 7

Butler paired his deuces. No one else improved. Tunney still had nines, Johnson fours, and Three-Eyed Jack received a useless six.

Tunney, still high with his nines, said, "I'm not afraid of you, Jack. You been too hot. I bet three hundred."

Johnson looked down at his fours, peeked at his hole cards, then said, "Ah, crap," and tossed his cards in.

Butler waited, then said, "Call."

"Your play, Jack," Coe said.

"Raise three hundred."

"Sonofabitch, I call!" Tunney said immediately. "I'm not lettin' you run me outta this hand, Jack."

"Good for you," Jack said. "I just hope three nines are good."

"Up to you, Butler," Coe said.

"I'll just call."

"Last card," Coe said, and dealt each man his seventh and last card.

Butler looked at his third hole card, then set it down. He looked across the table at Tunney, who was still the high man.

"Five hundred, damn it," Tunney said. "I bet five hundred."

Butler thought a moment. He wondered if Jack would still try to run Tunney out if he raised now. He knew Jack didn't have a royal, or a straight flush, but how was he going to bet? If he just called now would Jack raise?

"I raise," Butler said, "a thousand."

"What?" Tunney said. He'd been staring malevolently at Jack and now he jerked his head toward Butler. "I don't like this."

"I wouldn't think so," Jack said, with a smirk.

"What don't you like, John?" Coe asked.

"These two are workin' together," Tunney said, pointing to Butler and Jack in turn. "He's buildin' the pot for him."

"You sound like you don't think you have the winning hand," Three-Eyed Jack said. "What are you doin' in this pot, anyway?"

"Don't you worry," Tunney said. "I got the goods. I just don't like bein' worked by you two."

"There's no need for accusations, John," Dick Clark said.

"Hell, they know each other."

"Coe and I know each other," Clark said. "Are we workin' together?"

"Why else would he make a raise like that?" Tunney demanded.

"Maybe he thinks he's got a good hand," Clark said.

"He's got crap on the table."

"Why don't we play the hand out?" Jack asked.

"It's your play, Jack," Coe said.

"I just don't like it," Tunney muttered.

"You know," Coe said, "neither of these gentlemen is going to like being called a cheater."

"I think I'd rather be called a cheater," Jack said, "than be a sore loser."

"I ain't lost nothing yet!" Tunney said. "What're you doin', Jack, raisin' or callin'."

"In the face of that raise," Jack said, "I think I'll fold."

"What?" Tunney demanded.

"How could Butler be building a pot for Jack if Jack's going to fold?" Dick Clark asked Tunney.

"It's your play, Tunney," Coe said. "A thousand dollar raise to you."

"I reraise," Tunney said. "Two thousand."

"Raise," Butler said. "Two thousand."

Tunney's face turned red. He looked down at his money. He barely had two thousand left on the table.

"I call, damn it!" Tunney said. "Nobody's runnin' me outta this hand."

"You're called, Butler," Coe sad. "What do you have?"

"Deuces full of tens," Butler said. His hole cards were two deuces and the ten of hearts.

"Ten of hearts," Jack said, with a grin. "That's how you knew I didn't have a royal."

"And Coe folded the nine," Butler added, "so you couldn't have had a straight flush. Flush was the best you could do."

"And that's what I folded."

"Huh? Wha—you folded a flush?" Tunney asked.

"Sure," Jack said. "I figured with Butler raisin' like that, he knew I had a flush and didn't care."

"What do you have, Tunney?" Coe asked.

John Tunney looked around the table, saw that he was the center of attention, and turned even redder. He turned over his cards to show three nines.

"Lotta faith in three nines," Jack said.

"Butler wins the pot," Coe said.

"Nice hand, Butler," Clark said. "My deal. Tunney? You in or out?"

Tunney, glassy-eyed, looked around and said, "I—I'm out."

"We're back to five hands, then," Clark said. "Comin' out."

# CHAPTER 8

Without John Tunney the game went along much smoother. Three-Eyed Jack did, indeed, cool off and the hands began to go to Coe, Clark, and Butler a little more often. Jake Johnson was the next man to bust out of the game, leaving them four-handed for the rest of the night.

Butler hadn't realized the game would be an all-nighter but that was okay with him. Even though he'd ridden in that day, he was feeling fresh. Luke Short had a girl come up every so often with a pot of coffee, and one time even some sandwiches and hard-boiled eggs.

"Six A.M.," Charlie Coe announced eventually. "Anybody got anything to do today?"

"Sure," Dick Clark said. "I got a poker game to get to."

"Another one?" Coe asked.

"No, stupid, this one," Clark said. "I'm not goin' anywhere. I'm just startin' to warm up."

"You fellas?" Coe asked.

"I'm here for the duration," Jack said, "although I would like Luke to bring us some fresh meat."

"Butler?" Coe asked.

"I'm in."

"Anybody got any suggestions for Luke?" Dick Clark asked.

Nobody said anything, so Butler said, "I might have one . . ."

A couple of hours later Luke Short brought Al Newman into the room and introduced him to the other players. Newman gave Butler a look he correctly interpreted as "Thank you." He nodded.

"Hey, Luke," Coe said, "how about some breakfast."

"I'll have something set up on that table over there," Short said. "You fellas can decide if you want to eat at or away from the table."

Newman sat down and put his three thousand dollars on the table.

"All right," Clark said, "and we're back to five-handed."

"I'll keep lookin' for a sixth while I'm rustlin' you gents up some breakfast." Short spread his arms. "Anything else I can do for anyone?"

"Yeah, have some more coffee brought up right away," Coe said.

"Comin' up."

Short left, and Butler dealt out the next hand.

Newman got hot right away, Three-Eyed Jack played steady, Butler won as much as he lost, but both Coe and Clark went ice cold.

Coe had a full house that was beaten by Newman's four of a kind.

Dick Clark actually lost with a straight flush to a higher straight flush held by Butler.

That was when he really knew he was cold.

As Newman raked in yet another pot, Jack asked, "Who invited this guy?" Then, before Newman could get insulted, he added, "Nice hand, Al."

"Thanks, Jack."

The deal passed to Jack and he quickly shuffled the cards and announced, "Let's play a hand of draw poker, gents. I'm getting' tired of looking at all these face-up cards. I just want to look at my own."

Although they had been playing five- and seven-card stud since the day before, nobody objected.

Jack dealt each man five cards and they went around the table in turn.

Newman, sitting in the chair vacated by Tunney, said, "I open for a hundred."

"Call," Coe said,

Clark said, "Why doesn't that surprise me?" and followed with a call of his own.

"Butler?" Jack asked.

Butler was looking at a pat hand—he had three eights and two aces. It was sort of a reversed Deadman's Hand. He was wondering if he should call, or raise. Coe and Clark already had money in the pot, but Jack was still to make a play.

If he just called, not wanting to give away the strength of his hand, they'd all know he had a good hand when he didn't take any cards. It made more sense to see how much money he could get into the pot now.

"I raise two hundred," he said.

"Ah," Jack said, "we have a game. I call. One hundred to you, Al."

"I'll call."

"Charlie?"

"Call."

"Clark?"

"Against my better judgment," Dick Clark said, "I call."

"Well, gents," Jack said, "this has the look of an interesting hand. How many cards?"

# CHAPTER 9

———◆———

Al Newman drew two cards. No secrets there. He had three of a kind. He might have been keeping an Ace kicker. No pro would do that, but Newman was not a pro.

Coe drew one card, probably trying to fill a straight or a flush. Also could have had two pair.

Now it was Butler's turn.

"I'll play these."

That woke everybody up, although Coe looked the least surprised.

"I'm going to take three cards and hope for the best," Jack said.

More than likely he had a high pair, jack through aces, Butler figured. Although in Butler's mind if you were going to call with kings, why not call with, say, fives? You still have the potential of three or even four of a kind. Even four deuces was a powerhouse hand.

"All right, gents," Jack said. "We all have our cards. Let's see how we do against Butler's pat hand."

The play moved to Newman, who had opened and drawn two cards.

"I have to check to the power," he said, with a nod toward Butler.

Coe looked at his fanned cards, then folded them into his and said, "I check."

Butler knew Coe wanted to fold but couldn't do that until the play went around the table and somebody made a bet.

Now Butler had to make his bet. Nobody was going to want to go in against his pat hand, especially if he made a high bet. What he had to do was make a value bet—a bet that was not too high for someone to want to pay to see his cards. Considering the money in front of them on the table, either Jack or Newman might go ahead and pay to see them, just out of curiosity.

"I bet a thousand," Butler said.

"Hmm," Jack said. "That's not a very big bet for a pat hand. You're tryin' to tell us somethin'."

"What's he trying to tell us?" Al Newman asked.

"Here comes a poker lesson, courtesy of Three-Eyed Jack," Dick Clark said good-naturedly.

"He's tryin' to keep us in," Jack said. "Tryin' to get some money out of one of us. If he bets too high, we'll all fold, so he's making a value bet, hoping one of us will a least be curious enough to see the hand to pay.

"Or," Jack went on, "he bluffed a pat hand and doesn't want to risk a big bet on a bluff. If one of us raises back, he might fold."

"If he's bluffing that he has a pat hand, wouldn't he bet bigger to support that fact?" Newman asked. He was enjoying his time at the table, and that included all the poker lessons.

"He might," Jack said, "but this is Butler. I've played

with him before, and Charlie you've played with him for hours now. What do you think?"

Coe smiled.

"I think I'll wait my turn before I make my play, or even a comment."

"Touché," Jack said. "So the play is to me, and I fold to Butler's pat hand."

Newman stared across the table at Butler, and at his hand.

"Okay, I'm the donkey," Newman said. "I want to see his cards, so I call."

"I fold," Charlie Coe said quickly. "Even if Butler doesn't have a pat hand I can't beat your three of a kind, Al."

"Butler," Jack said, "you're called."

Butler laid out his hand and they all saw the full house.

"Nice," Clark said.

Newman showed his hand, three jacks.

"Full house wins," Jack said. "Very nice hand, Butler."

"I know," Newman said, putting up his hands, "I wasted a thousand dollars.

"Hey, nobody's judging your play, Al," Dick Clark said.

"Did you want to see his hand?" Coe asked.

"Very much."

"Then your money wasn't wasted."

"Unless Butler would have shown his hand anyway," Newman pointed out.

Before Butler could respond, Jack said, "Oh, no, with Butler you have to pay to see his hand."

"That's the way the game should be played," Charlie Coe said. "If you want to know somebody's hand without payin' for it, ask them later, away from the table. Believe me, every poker player remembers every hand."

"A poker lesson courtesy of Dick Clark," Jack said.

Coe looked at Jack, smiled and said, "Touché."

# CHAPTER 10

———◆———

Luke Short set out a dinner for them on a table against the wall. As with the other meals, each player had wandered over during the game, eaten something or taken it back to the table. This time when they broke, all moved to the table to eat and have a drink. Butler limited himself to one beer. He noticed Charlie Coe and Dick Clark had two whiskeys each and then a beer. Three-Eyed Jack had three beers. Al Newman drank half a beer, apparently just to wash down the food.

"How long do these games go on?" Newman asked, during the break.

"I can't tell you," Butler said. "Sometimes hours, sometimes days. When I sat down here yesterday I had no idea it would go this long."

"By the way, thanks for getting me in the game," Newman said. "I know it was you who spoke to Luke on my behalf."

"Hey, we were down to four-handed. Everybody just wanted another body."

"Okay, yeah," Newman said. "I still say thanks."

"Forget it," Butler said. "I'm going to do my best to take all your money."

"Thanks for the warning. But tell me, if I hadn't called you on that hand, would you have shown it?"

"I never show my hand for free," Butler said. "Somebody's got to pay."

"You know," Newman said, "I used to think I was a good poker player, but I'm learning a lot here."

"Good," Butler said, "just don't use too much of what you've learned on me."

The game went on into the night, with Luke Short stopping in to see how everyone was doing. Butler thought Short was not only surprised to see that Al Newman was still in the game, but that he was flourishing. Three-Eyed Jack, who'd had the hot hand for so long, until Butler joined the game, and then Newman, finally had his luck take a turn for the worse. Charlie Coe and Dick Clark were playing pretty even, and Butler had the feeling they were almost done. Treading water for a few days was not worth the effort.

Butler was well ahead, and Al Newman was winning

Just as Butler predicted, around three A.M. Charlie Coe announced that he was finished.

"This is ridiculous," he said. "After the better part of three days I'm even. Time for me to move on. Gents, it's been a pleasure."

He stood up, shook hands with everybody, and took his leave.

"So are we playin' four-handed?" Dick Clark asked, looking around the table.

"Sure, why not?" Jack said. "I'm game."

"Although if I don't start winning some pots soon, I'm going to have to call it quits, too," Clark said. "I know how Charlie feels. After all this time I'm close to even, too. It's not a good feelin'."

As it turned out there had been several other players in and out of the game before Butler joined in who had donated their money to the cause. There were virtually no losers at the table at the moment—although Three-Eyed Jack had given back quite a bit of what he'd won the first two days.

"Okay," Jack said, "we're four-handed. The game is five-card stud."

# CHAPTER 11

By seven A.M. Dick Clark was ready to quit, Jack had fallen into a hole. Al Newman was ahead, and Butler was the big winner. With players moving in and out of the game there had been eleven overall. With a three thousand dollar buy-in that put better than thirty-three thousand dollars in play—depending on how many players had bought in for more than that—and Butler had more than half of that.

"You were bad luck for me, Butler," Three-Eyed Jack said good-naturedly. "My luck went south when you sat down."

"Ever think I just outplayed you, Jack?" Butler asked. "Or that you were too hot for too long and just burned out?"

Jack thought for a moment, and then said, "I don't like either one of those. I prefer to think you were bad luck for me."

They all began taking their jackets off the back of their chairs, tucking money away in their wallets, buttoning their shirts.

"I need a long bath," Butler said.

"I think we all do," Dick Clark said. "Where are you stayin'?"

"Up the street," Butler said. "A place called the Wisteria, whatever that means."

"I think it's a plant," Al Newman said. "It's also a very good hotel."

"Somebody's got to let Luke know we're done," Clark said. "He'll want to lock this room."

"I'll find him," Butler said. "I want to thank him for bringing me into a game with such easy pickings."

"You're not leaving town, are you?" Dick Clark asked.

"Are you kidding?" Butler asked. "I may never leave."

"Good, I'll be here awhile, we can have another go at it."

"Any time," Butler said.

"Jack?"

"I'm supposed to head out," Three-Eyed Jack said, "but after this I may need to rest up. I'm not as young as I used to be."

"You ready for some more, Al?" Dick Clark asked.

Al Newman seemed very pleased to be asked and said, "Just name the time."

"We'll set it up with Luke and let you know," Clark promised.

They all left the room together, made their way down a hall and came out into the casino, which at that time of the morning was empty.

"I've never seen this room like this," Dick Clark said.

"It's so quiet," Newman said.

All the gaming tables were covered and the bar was closed. They went down the long stairway to the main floor and found the same to be true there.

"Luke is probably in his bed," Dick Clark said. "His wife probably wouldn't take too kindly to us wakin' him—and her."

"You're probably right," Butler said. "I'll come by later and see him."

However, when they made their way to the front door they found a man sleeping in a chair. He was wearing a gun and had his hat pulled down over his eyes.

"I think this is our man," Butler said. "He's probably here to lock the doors after we leave."

"I hate to wake him," Jack said.

"You already did," the man said. He pushed his hat up off his eyes and squinted up at them. "You the fellers were in the private game?"

"That's right," Clark said. "The game's over."

"Okay," he said, getting to his feet. "I'll lock up behind ya."

"Thanks," Clark said. "Let Luke know we appreciate it."

"I'll tell 'im." The man yawned widely.

"What's your name?" Butler asked.

"I'm Victor," the man said. "Just Victor."

"Well, get some sleep, Victor," Butler said. "Sorry to have to wake you."

"No problem," Victor assured them. "This is what I get paid for."

Outside Newman asked, "Anybody for breakfast? I know a great place just down the street."

"As the only player who lives here, I'll bet you do,"

Butler said. "I'll take you up on that offer."

"Not me," Dick Clark said. "I'm turnin' in."

"Me too," Jack said. "These old bones need rest."

"'Night, gents," Newman said. "Thanks again for the game—and the lessons."

"Seems to me you learned your lessons pretty well, Al," Jack told him.

"Good night," Clark said.

"How far we going?" Butler asked Newman.

"Like I said, just down the street, this way."

"Lead on, then," Butler said. "I'm almost as hungry as I am tired."

# CHAPTER 12

———◆———

The restaurant Newman took Butler to was packed with people eating breakfast. There was not a table with less than four diners at it. Apparently, the Stockyard was every bit as good as Newman had promised—so good that the locals flocked to it.

"When you said it was good," Butler said, "you didn't mention how popular it was."

"I'm sorry," Newman said, "I guess it's not as early as I thought. We'll have to wait."

But there was one table with only two people at it, and Luke Short stood up and waved at them.

"I guess we won't have to wait," Butler said, pointing.

They walked over to where Short was sitting with his partner, Bill Ward. Newman knew Ward, of course, so Short introduced Butler, and the two men sat down and joined the partners.

"You fellas called it a game, huh?" Short asked.

"I guess it was about time," Butler said. "Coe and Clark and Jack were at it a lot longer than we were."

"Lot of people in and out of that game," Short said. "How'd you boys do?"

"Very well," Butler said.

"I did okay," Newman said.

"He did better than okay," Butler added. "He held his own and then some."

"Who was the big loser?" Ward asked.

"Since I didn't see all the players involved, I don't know that," Butler said, "but I can tell you who the biggest sore loser was."

"Tunney," Short said.

"You got it right," Butler said. "How did you know?"

"I saw him on his way out," Short answered. "He was not happy. Said he thought you and Jack were playin' partners."

"What did you tell him?"

"I told him to get out of my place and not come back," Short said.

"You didn't," Ward said.

"I did."

"John Tunney loses a lot of money in our place, Luke," Ward pointed out.

"Not anymore," Short said.

"We better talk about this later," Ward said, obviously not wanting to discuss business in front of Butler and Newman.

"We can talk about it now, Bill," Short said. "The man accused two of my people of cheating. I don't tolerate that."

"Your people?" Ward said. "You never even wanted to give Al here a chance to play. Now, all of a sudden, he's your people?"

Butler was watching Newman when Short said "my

people" and it obviously pleased him. Now, after hearing what Bill Ward had to say, he looked crestfallen.

"Bill, now that Al has played in my game and acquitted himself well, yes, he's one of my people. And you wanted me to buy into the White Elephant so that I would bring my people in, right?"

"That's true, but I didn't want you chasing other people out."

"Believe me," Short said, "Tunney didn't gamble so much that I can't replace him."

"Luke, damn it—""

"You know what?" Short said. "You're right."

"I am?" Ward looked shocked. Obviously, he did not win a lot of arguments with Luke Short.

"Yes," Short said, "we should talk about this later."

Short and Ward had just put in their orders for breakfast, so Butler and Newman were able to order theirs in time for all four plates to come at the same time. Newman assured Butler that steak and eggs was the specialty, and since that's what everyone was ordering, he just made it four.

Through the conversation Butler learned that Newman was retired. He no longer practiced law unless it was as a favor to a friend. He lived in a small house in a modest section of town, even though he could have afforded a better place. It was the house where his first wife had died, and he could not bring himself to leave. It all sounded a little bit morbid to Butler, but he didn't make a comment.

The steak was so tender it almost melted when Butler

put his knife to it. The eggs were perfectly prepared, and the potatoes were crisp and delicious. To top it all off, the coffee was excellent. So far, Butler had found the best places in town to stay, to gamble, and to eat, and he said so.

"Now you just need to find the best place in town for a woman," Short said.

"Don't tell me—""

"No," Short said, cutting him off, "we are not running women upstairs in the White Elephant. Bill is way too moral to let me do that."

"There are enough brothels in Fort Worth," Ward said. "We're not about that."

"No, we're not," Short said. "We're all about the gambling."

"And we have an excellent restaurant of our own," Ward added.

"Steaks as good as these?" Butler asked.

"Well, no . . . but the food is good."

"He's right," Short said, "we do serve good food. It could be better, though. We're looking for a new cook."

"We are?" Ward asked.

Short patted the man's arm and said, "Later, Bill."

Butler didn't know if he could be partners with a man as condescending as Short was to Bill Ward. He did not see a long and happy future for this partnership.

After breakfast all four men exited the restaurant together, with the same idea.

"Time to get some rest," Short said. "We've got to open in a few hours and start it all over again."

"Thanks again for allowing me to play, Luke," Newman said, shaking hands with the man.

"Don't thank me, Al," Short said. "This puts you in my debt, and someday soon I may want to collect."

Later, Butler would recall just how prophetic that statement was.

# CHAPTER 13

Over the next few days another poker game of grand proportions did not come together. Butler played in a couple of games that petered out after he won most of the money.

On the fourth day he was in the White Elephant, standing at the bar, when Short came walking over to him.

"Looks like Bat was right about you," he said.

"Right about what?"

"You're scaring off the competition," Short said. "By all accounts you're a helluva poker player."

"I'm sure you can put a game together with all your connections."

"I have a few fellas comin' to town that may interest you," Short said.

"Oh? Who?"

"Let's wait until they actually get here," Short said. "Just stay around at least a couple more days. See the sights of Fort Worth."

"I've been around town," Butler said.

"Just don't go into any of those downtown places,"

Short said. "The city fathers are up in arms about gambling halls skinnin' customers, and it's none of our doin'. It's those damned places. I ought to go down there and shoot a couple of them up."

"Is that wise?"

"No, damn it, it ain't," Short said. "But it's what I want to do. Hey." He lit up like he just had a great idea. "Why don't you come with me?"

"To shoot the places up."

"No, I'm havin' a meetin' down there this afternoon with a fella called Cramer. We got some business together. Come along."

"Why would you want me in on your business?"

"Bat said you do a pretty fair job of watchin' a fella's back," Short said. "I'm goin' to Hell's Half Acre— which, by the way, covers more like three acres. I think I need someone I can count on behind me."

"I'm flattered that you'd think of me, Luke," Butler said. "Sure, I'd be happy to go with you. Am I going to need my horse?"

"We can take a cab," Short said. "Actually, we could probably walk it, but I think a cab would be better. I'll have one out front at three o'clock. Meet me then, okay?"

"Three o'clock, out front," Butler said. "I'll be there."

Butler made it back to the White Elephant early, so he went to the bar for a beer. The bartender who greeted him the first night came over with a smile.

"Whataya have, Mr. Butler?"

"How do you know my name?"

"Mr. Short made me memorize it," the man said, "but I had it after the first time."

"And what's your name?"

"I'm Jerry."

"Well, Jerry, I'll have one of those cold beers that freeze your hand."

"Comin' up."

Jerry went down the bar and returned with a frosty mug.

"Heard you and the boss were going to the Acre."

"Word gets around fast."

"Well, when somebody hates those places as much as Mr. Short does . . . You gonna help him shoot them up?"

"Nobody's going to shoot any place up, Jerry," Butler said. "I'm just going to watch his back."

"Well, he's gonna need it if you go there," Jerry said. "Especially if he's goin' to see Cramer."

"He mentioned a man named Cramer."

"Yeah, he owns a few of those places downtown that are fleecin' people," Jerry said. "Mr. Short hates that. He likes to run a straight game. He don't like when we get lumped in with those places in the newspapers."

"I can't blame him for that," Butler said, "but we're still not going to shoot any place up."

"Well, maybe you can keep him from doin' it," Jerry said. "'Scuse me. More customers. Place is startin' to fill up now."

Butler turned around with his beer in hand and saw that Jerry was right. The gaming tables were starting to fill up, and he wondered how things were going up in the casino. He knew Luke Short was running the casino upstairs, but he wondered if the dapper little gambler also had a piece of the few downstairs games. Wouldn't seem worth his while, since most of the players at these games were penny-ante locals.

He was half finished with the beer when he checked his watch and saw it was almost three. He didn't know if he was supposed to watch Luke's back or keep him from getting into trouble, but whichever it was he was ready.

# CHAPTER 14

In the cab, Luke Short gave Butler a brief history of Fort Worth's downtown, alternately called Hell's Half Acre and the Bloody Third Ward.

"Originally it was limited to Rusk Street, or the lower half of it, anyway, but lately it's grown to include other streets like Main, Calhoun, and Jones. From north to south it covers Front to Seventh Street. The *Fort Worth Democrat* claims it now covers two-and-a-half acres."

Butler didn't tell Short that he'd already heard some of this from Jerry the bartender.

"It pisses me off when we get included in what the newspapers are decrying the Acre," Short went on. "The White Elephant is nothing like these places."

"What are we doing here, Luke?" Butler asked.

"I'm having a meeting with a man named Ed Cramer," Short said, "not to be confused with my friend Nat Kramer, who runs the Cattle Exchange Saloon on Houston Street. Do you know Nat has never carried a gun, and has never had occasion to need one? I don't know how he does it."

"Who knows?" Butler asked. "Maybe if we didn't carry them we wouldn't need them, either."

Short laughed and said, "If I didn't wear my gun I'd be dead in ten minutes."

"You're probably right," Butler said. With the price that was still on his head, put there not by the law but by a private citizen, he probably wouldn't last much longer than that.

The cab pulled to a stop in front of a building on Rusk Street. As they alighted to the street Butler saw the name, the Bloody Spur Saloon, over the door.

"Nice name," he commented.

"Actually," Short said, "that is one of the nicer-named places down here."

The traffic on Rusk Street looked the same as any other street Butler had seen in Fort Worth. However, he'd been to enough red-light districts to know that the trouble started when the sun went down.

"Let's go inside," Short said. "I have an appointment to talk to Cramer in about ten minutes. He'll keep me waiting at least that long."

"What's this about?"

"I heard some rumors that Cramer has hired someone to harass our customers, maybe even come to our place and cause trouble. I want to try to cut him off at the pass, so to speak. Reason with him."

"Is he a reasonable man?"

"Never has been before," Short said, "but one can always hope. Just keep your eyes peeled for trouble while I do the talkin'."

"Gotcha."

They entered the place, attracted the eyes of several

customers who were lounging against the bar. It was much smaller than the White Elephant—probably a quarter of the size—and the furnishings were unremarkable. In fact, the clientele appeared as rundown as the furniture and bar. And then there was the smell . . .

"Jesus," Short said, as the odor struck him.

"Yeah."

The closest Butler could come to identifying it was vomit and sweat. He didn't understand how anyone could drink, or even sit, in the place.

"They're used to it," Short said, as if reading his mind.

"How?"

Short shrugged, led the way to the bar.

"Would you tell your boss Luke Short is here to see him?" he asked the bartender.

"Sure thing," the man said. "You got an appointment?" He laughed, showing rotted stumps where his teeth used to be.

"As a matter of fact, I do," Short said.

That seemed to disappoint the man, whose laughter abruptly stopped.

"I'll tell 'im," he said, and left the bar.

"Don't have a drink in here," Short whispered to Butler.

"You don't have to tell me twice."

The bartender walked to the back and went through a curtained doorway. Moments later he reappeared with another man. This one was much better dressed than anyone else in the place, but his suit did not come close to matching the caliber of Luke Short's or Butler's.

"Hey, Luke, good to see you." He approached with his hand held out for a handshake. Butler detected some hesitation in Short, who finally did shake hands.

"How are you, Ed?"

"Can't complain. Who's your friend?" Cramer gave Butler a critical once over.

"Friend of mine named Butler," Short said. "I brought him to the Acre to see how the other half lives."

Cramer laughed.

"Always the joker, Luke. You wanna come back to my office and talk?" Cramer asked.

"Why don't we just take a table near the back," Short suggested.

"Sure, Luke," Cramer said. "You wanna stay out in the open, we can do that. How about your friend? Does he want to come along?"

"No, he'll stay at the bar."

"Fine. Hey, Zeke, give the man what he wants on the house."

"What'll ya have?" the bartender asked as Short and Cramer walked to the back.

"Whiskey," Butler said.

A least it would come from a bottle, and the liquor would kill whatever was in the glass—not that he intended to drink it.

Butler noticed another doorway, this one way in the corner. He thought he saw part of a stairway. He also thought he saw a shadow. He decided to keep a wary eye on that spot. Cramer probably just had his own backup, there was no harm in that.

Yet.

# CHAPTER 15

The conversation between Cramer and Short seemed to start out amiably enough, but soon Short was getting red in the face. Butler was impressed that Cramer seemed to be keeping his composure.

"Your boss keeps that up he's gonna have a heart attack," Zeke the bartender said.

"He's not my boss," Butler said. "We're friends."

"Yeah, right."

Butler decided it didn't matter what the bartender thought. He kept an eye on the two men at the table, and on that doorway in the corner.

"What's over there?" he asked Zeke.

"Where?"

"That doorway." Butler pointed.

"Oh," Zeke said. "Stairway to upstairs."

"What's upstairs?"

Zeke grinned, showing more of his yellow and black stumps, and said, "Girls. You want one?"

"Not from here."

"Best in town."

"I'll pass."

"You want a boy?" Zeke asked. "You one of them? We got them, too."

"I don't think your boys would be any cleaner than your girls, do you?" Butler asked.

"You sayin' we got diseased whores here?"

"I'm saying," Butler replied, "that you probably have diseased whores here, yes."

"And I suppose the whores at the White Elephant are all clean, huh?"

"There are no whores at the White Elephant," Butler said.

"Yeah, right," the bartender said again.

Butler decided it was useless talking to the man, but the bartender wouldn't leave him alone.

"You gonna drink that?" the man asked, indicating the whiskey. "Or afraid that's dirty, too?

"Yes."

The man grabbed the glass and drained it himself, then put it back with the other glasses without washing or even wiping it.

Suddenly, there was some commotion from the corner. Luke Short stood up so fast his chair fell over. Cramer sat back in his chair and smiled, spreading his hands to show Short he wasn't armed. Some of the customers looked over there but lost interest quickly.

Zeke put his hand under the bar.

"You come up with a gun I'm going to shove it up your ass," Butler said.

Zeke pulled his hand back as if he'd touched something very hot.

Butler now had to watch Short, the bartender, and the doorway to the stairs. As Short's voice got louder—

Butler heard him call Cramer a "sonofabitch and whoremonger,"—Butler saw the shadow in the stairway move, and then the barrel of a gun poked out.

"Don't make a move," he told Zeke as he pushed away from the bar. "Nobody has to get hurt here."

He quickly crossed the room, and as a hand appeared holding the gun he grabbed it by the wrist and yanked. The man came stumbling out of the stairway and, as he did, Butler drew his gun, pressing it to the man's temple.

"Drop it."

"I didn't do nothin'."

"Sure," Butler said, "you always walk around with a gun in your hand."

The man opened his hand and his gun hit the floor. Butler kicked it across the room.

"Go stand with your friend at the bar," he ordered.

The man walked across the room and stood in front of the bar. Butler stayed where he was, because from there he could cover the whole room. He stole a look up the stairway, but there was nobody there.

"Clear, Luke," he said.

"Is that what you had planned for me?" Short demanded of Cramer. "Bushwackin' me?"

"I didn't have anything to do with that, Luke," Cramer claimed.

Short pulled his gun, put his knee against Cramer's chest and pressed the barrel against the man's lips.

"Open up, you sonofabitch," he said.

Slowly, Cramer opened his mouth and Short slid his gun barrel in.

"You send anybody to the White Elephant to even spit

on the floor," he said, "I'll come back here and blow the back of your head out. You understand? Nod your head if you do, but not too hard. This is a hair trigger. I don't want to kill you accidentally."

Cramer nodded very slowly.

Short slid the gun out of his mouth, but kept the hammer cocked.

"Cover me, Butler," Short said. "When I get to the door I'll cover you."

"Right."

Butler kept the room covered, even though he thought the only two he had to worry about were the men at the bar. Cramer was still sitting in his chair, looking remarkably calm.

"Okay," Short said, and covered Butler as he crossed the room.

"Remember what I said, Ed," Short told Cramer.

"I'll remember everything that happened here today, Luke," Cramer promised.

Butler and Short backed out through the batwing doors. Once outside Short holstered his gun.

"He won't come out after us?" Butler asked.

"No," Short said, "he'll send somebody else to do his fightin' for him. Come on, let's get a ways from here before we get a cab."

Once Short and Butler were out of the saloon, Cramer's man ran across the room and picked up his gun. As he started for the door Cramer stopped him.

"But they're gettin' away, boss."

"You'll just get yourself killed, Martin," Cramer said. "You let that tinhorn gambler get the drop on you."

"He ain't so—"

"Shut up," Cramer said. "I want to know who that gambler is. I want to know all about him. Where he came from, what he's doing here, and how long he's going to be in town."

"I can do that, boss," Martin said.

"Not you, you idiot," Cramer said. "Find me Sutherland."

"Sutherland?" Martin asked. "I can do anythin' he can do, boss."

"No, Martin, you can't," Cramer said, "because after I find out who that fella was, I want him dead."

"I can do—"

"Martin," Cramer said, cutting him off, "you have not filled me with confidence today—"

"Boss—"

"—so shut the hell up, and go find me Sutherland—now!"

# CHAPTER 16

When they were in a cab, on their way back to the White Elephant, Short said, "Thanks, Butler. I knew I made the right decision takin' you with me."

"What was that all about?"

"That was about Ed Cramer bein' a complete asshole, like he always is," Short said. "I don't know why I thought I'd be able to talk to him. He gets under my skin every time."

"How do you know him? From here?"

"Cramer and I have been in the same place at the same time in a few different towns," Short said, "but this is the first time we both own a place in the same town. And it ain't workin'."

"Well," Butler said, "at least we didn't end up shooting the place up."

"Oh, crap," Short said.

"What?"

"I knew I forgot to do something'."

When they got back to the White Elephant, Butler went to the bar for a drink. Short told him he had to go to the office to talk to his partner, Ward, and that he'd see him later.

"I'm gonna buy you a meal."

"You don't have to—"

"It's the least I can do," Short said. "Meet me here at six."

"Okay," Butler said, "six."

As Short walked away, Jerry came over with a beer and said to Butler, "Fireworks?"

"Not even a spark."

Jerry looked disappointed.

"Not even one shot?"

"No," Butler said, "but Luke did put his gun into Ed Cramer's mouth and threaten to blow the back of his head out."

"Awright," Jerry said. "I knew there'd be some excitement."

"Just a little."


Luke Short told Bill Ward what had happened in Hell's Half Acre with Ed Cramer.

"Damn it, Luke," Ward said. "Don't you have enough enemies? Don't we?"

"Cramer's an old enemy of mine, Bill," Short said. "This is nothin' new."

"Well, it's new for me," Ward said. "Did you go there alone? You could've been killed."

"No, I took Butler," Short said. "He saved my bacon once already."

"Then he's a good man to have around."

"That's what I was thinkin'."

"What, you want to hire him?"

"Yes."

"To do what?"

"Whatever he wants," Short said. "To gamble here. Just to be around."

"Is he a name that's going to draw other gamblers?" Ward asked.

Short smiled.

"By the time I'm done," he said, confidently, "he will be."

"Go ahead, then," Ward said. "And what about those rumors that Cramer's going to send someone over here to start trouble? Did you . . . convince him it wouldn't be wise?"

"He's a stubborn cuss. But he won't be sendin' anyone for a while."

"Why not?"

"First he's going to have to do some askin' about Butler, find out who he is, where he came from," Short said. "That'll take a few days."

"Then what?"

"Then he'll probably send someone to try and kill him," Short said, "or me, or both."

"Does Butler know all this?"

"He's a smart man," Short said. "I'm sure he can figure it out."

"That's why you invited him to go with you?" Ward asked. "And why you want to hire him, to use him as . . . as bait?"

"No," Short said. "That's not why I took him with me. It occurred to me later."

"So having him here is going to draw Cramer out?" Ward asked.

"Havin' him and me here is gonna do that."

"And then what?"

"That's up to Cramer," Short said, "or whoever he sends."

# CHAPTER 17

"Sit down," Ed Cramer said to Kale Sutherland.

The gunman sat.

"Did you hear that Luke Short was here earlier today?" Cramer asked.

"I heard," Sutherland said. "And I heard what he did."

"I don't want to talk about that," Cramer said.

Sutherland shrugged.

"You're the boss."

That was why Cramer liked Sutherland, and why he used him.

"He had a man with him," Cramer said, "a gambler named Butler. Do you know him?"

"No."

"Never heard of him?"

"No."

"He took one of my men," Cramer sad, "disarmed him pretty easily. Intimidated Zeke."

"That don't sound too hard."

"I want to know who he is," Cramer said. "I want to know everything about him before I have you kill him."

"All right."

"And then, not until I give the word."

"Okay."

"How long will it take?" Cramer asked. "Gathering this information."

"I got to send some telegrams," Sutherland said. "Check some contacts. Probably a few days."

"Fine," Cramer said.

"What about our plans for the White Elephant?" Sutherland asked.

"Stay away from there for a while," Cramer said. "And keep your men away. I'll give the go-ahead when the time comes."

"That it?"

"That's all."

Sutherland stood up, but didn't leave.

"What?" Cramer asked.

"When am I gonna get the okay to take a run at Luke Short?"

"Soon," Cramer said, "very soon, Sutherland."

"Can't be soon enough for me," the gunman said, and left.

# CHAPTER 18

Luke Short took Butler to eat in the White Elephant's restaurant. Butler felt it was probably to prove the food was decent. He decided not to order steak. The place might suffer by comparison. Instead, he ordered a bowl of beef stew, which came piping hot with big chunks of meat and vegetables, and a basket of biscuits.

Luke Short had chicken.

"How is it?" he asked, pointing to the beef stew with his fork.

"Very good." It was passable, at best, but Butler didn't want to say so.

"I want to offer you a job," Short said. "I want you on the payroll."

"To do what?"

"Gamble," Short said. "Play poker here."

"You think I'm going to draw anyone? You need Bat, or Doc, or Ben Thompson for that."

"Word will get around," Short said. "We'll get some comers."

"And that's all you want me to do? Gamble?"

"No," Short said. "I want you to do what you did today. Watch my back."

"You think Cramer will move against you?"

"As soon as—" he stopped himself.

"As soon as he checks me out," Butler said.

"I'm sorry but, yes, he will check you out. You took two of his men out of the play this afternoon, and you saw him embarrassed."

"So he's going to come after me?"

"Likely, he'll send somebody for both of us."

"Any idea who?"

"There's a few men I can think of," Short said, "but he'll import some talent to lead them."

"I'm not a gunman, Luke."

"You don't have to be a gunman to handle a gun, Butler," Short said. "I'm not hirin' your gun. I'm hirin' the whole package. All your talents."

"Talents," Butler said. "I've really only got two."

"What are those?"

"Poker," Butler said, "and getting myself wrapped in other people's problems."

"Yeah, Bat told me that about you, too."

Over dessert Short asked, "So whataya say?"

"I suppose I could stay around for a while."

"Good," Short said. "Let's talk about salary."

"Whatever you think is fair," Butler said, "but I get to keep all my winnings, right?"

"Definitely," Short said. "I don't want a cut of anything. I just want you around."

"Why not send for Bat? Or Wyatt?"

"They've got their own lives," Short said. "Sure, if

they walked through the front door I'd press them into service, but I'm not going to put out a call for help. Not until I'm sure you and me can't handle what comes along."

"There's one other thing I want before I say yes."

"Oh? What's that?"

"You've got to promise me you'll sit down at a poker table with me, at least once, before I leave."

"You want to test yourself against me?"

"I want to test myself against the best," Butler said. "You know anybody else fits that description?"

Luke Short smiled and said, "Okay, you got a deal."

# CHAPTER 19

Now that Butler was on salary, Short offered him a room in the White Elephant, but he declined.

"I like where I am, and now that you're paying me it's almost like you're footing the bill."

"You've got a point," Short said.

When they finished their meal they walked into the saloon.

"I've got to go upstairs and make sure everything is running smooth," Short said.

"I'll be around," Butler said. "I don't think you need me to be up your ass right now."

"No," Short said. "We've got Victor on the door. You met Victor, right?"

"Oh, right. He locked up after us. We thought he was asleep, but . . ."

"That's Victor," Short said. "He's a lot more observant than people give him credit for."

"How's he with a gun?"

"Fair," Short said, "just fair. But you can count on him in a fight."

"Good to know. Anybody else?"

"I made sure our bartenders were good at more than just pouring drinks. Jerry you met, one of the others is Billy Catlett. Look to either of them if anything goes wrong."

"Okay," Butler said. "One more thing. Who's the law in town?"

"That'd be Jim Courtwright," Short said. "They call him Long-haired Jim. He and I don't get along real good, but he seems to do his job."

Short went up to the casino and Butler walked to the door, where Victor was still sitting like last time he'd seen him.

"I hear you're on the payroll," Victor said. "Glad to have ya."

He put out his hand and Butler shook it.

"Heard you're pretty good with a deck of cards," Victor said. "But how about a gun?"

"I get by."

"That's good, because ain't worth shit with a hogleg. Can't hit the side of a barn."

"We all have our strengths," Butler said.

"Yeah, mine's noticin' things," Victor said, "and breakin' heads."

"I'll keep that in mind if I need any heads broken," Butler said. "What do you know about the sheriff, Jim Courtwright?"

Victor made a face.

"Don't like 'im, but I don't get along much with any law, so ya can't go by me."

"Let me know when he comes in, will you?" Butler asked. "Or anybody else you think looks a little suspicious."

"I know most of Ed Cramer's men," Victor said. "I see any of them, should I stop 'em?"

"Yes," Butler said, "and then see if you can find Luke or me."

"Gotcha," Victor said. "Good to have you on board, Butler."

Butler left Victor at the door and made a circuit of the room. He didn't know what he was looking for, except maybe something out of the ordinary. The penny-ante gamblers were throwing away their money, concentrating half on the game and half on drinking or flirting with the saloon girls.

Butler didn't have a title, but he figured Short had signed him on as a troubleshooter. When he wasn't playing in a poker game—like now, when there was no high-stakes game—he figured he'd just keep his eyes open.

At one point he ran into Bill Ward, who also seemed to be walking the floor, making sure everything was going along smoothly.

"Butler."

"Mr. Ward."

"Naw, naw," Ward said. "Since you're on our payroll now, you can just call me Bill. Seen Luke?"

"Last I saw him he was going upstairs."

Ward shook his head.

"He loves it up there," Ward said.

"Looks like you picked the right partner."

"You and Luke just met, right?" Ward asked.

"That's right."

"Heard you had a little blow up with Ed Cramer today. Luke start that?"

"Luke was just sitting at a table talking to Cramer when a fella with a gun came down the stairs."

"Was he wearing it?"

Butler shook his head.

"Had it in his hand."

"There was no shooting?"

Was Ward double-checking the facts that Luke Short had given him?

Butler shook his head.

"I took it away from him."

"Then what?"

"Then Luke warned Cramer to keep his people away from here," Butler said. "Bill, are you checking to see if my story matches up with Luke's?"

"No, no," Ward said. "Well, maybe. Luke's been known to play fast and loose with the truth when it suits him. He's done wonders for this place, really brought the gaming part to life, but . . ."

"Trouble follows him?"

"I'm afraid so," Ward said, "and I'm afraid Luke doesn't know how to back away from it."

"Bill, for men like Luke Short, Bat Masterson, Wyatt Earp—"

"You?"

"I'm not in that company," Butler said. "But for men like them, backing away from trouble isn't an option. They tend to meet it head on."

"My point exactly," Ward said. "I think push is going to come to shove between Luke and Ed Cramer, or Luke and Jim Courtwright. I just hope Luke comes out of it okay when it happens."

"And doesn't drag you and the White Elephant down?"

"I know that's the last thing Luke would ever do—" Ward said.

"You've got that right."

"—on purpose."

# CHAPTER 20

Everything was quiet for several days. Still no high-stakes game for Butler. If he hadn't been on the White Elephant's payroll he might have left town for lack of action.

And why was he on the payroll, he wondered? What he had told Luke Short was the truth. He did often stick his nose in other people's business—but he had come out of those situations with some lasting friendships. Hopefully, that was what would happen here. On the other hand, people had also died.

Not only was it three days of no poker, but three days of no action of any kind. There hadn't even been an argument in the saloon, or the casino, and when men got together to drink and gamble, there were always arguments.

Over supper in the White Elephant restaurant on day four, Butler said, "Has it ever been this quiet?"

"No," Short said, "and that's what worries me. When it's this quiet it's bound to change with a bang."

"Maybe," Butler said, "you really did make an impression on Cramer. You know, with your gun?"

"No chance," Short said. "I don't even know why I did it, except that I was mad. All I did was make him even more stubborn. It's real easy to send someone to do your killing for you."

"Then why hasn't he?" Butler asked. "He's had time to check me out."

"All I know is the longer he takes, the more anxious I get."

"Maybe that's what he wants."

"What?"

"To make us anxious," Butler said, "jumpy. He wants us jumping at shadows."

"You're right," Short said, "that's just what he wants. Poor Bill Ward is a nervous wreck."

"Well," Butler said, "we just have to keep waiting. We can't make the first move."

"Why not?"

"We'd be in the wrong."

"Not if we didn't get caught."

"So what are you talking about doing, bushwacking Ed Cramer?

"No," Short said, "I'd never do that. You're right. We have to wait."

"And be on our toes."

"I'll talk to Victor and the boys," Short said. "The 'boys' being the bartenders. We can't have them getting careless." Short hesitated, then added, "Careless is dead."

Ed Cramer looked up as Sutherland came through the curtain into his office.

"You got him?" Cramer asked.

"I think so," Sutherland said. "If it's the same Butler, he's worth a lot of money back East."

"How much?"

Sutherland dropped the telegram on Cramer's desk, then sat down. Cramer picked it up and read.

"That is a lot of money. Is this a legal bounty?"

"No," Sutherland said, "best I can find out is that it's private, from out of the East. I guess that's where he comes from."

"So, Mr. Butler has gotten a rich man from the East angry enough to put a price on his head."

"Apparently Butler's family was pretty prominent, active in politics, wealthy, and got on somebody's wrong side. They're all dead except for him."

"So he's on the run."

"Seems like it."

"Well," Cramer said, "this is an extra bonus."

"Meaning you want a piece of the reward?"

"That's not just a reward, Sutherland," Cramer said, "that's a good year in this damn place. Why? Did you think it would be yours?"

"It occurred to me to claim it," Sutherland said. "After all, we're not partners. You're payin' me to do a job. Anythin' I pick up along the way—"

"Okay, how about this?" Cramer asked. "We'll be partners in this."

"Fifty-fifty?" Sutherland asked.

"Well, I want to be fair," Cramer said. "Since you're going to pull the trigger, why don't we make it sixty-forty . . . in your favor?"

"But you're still gonna pay me."

"Yes."

"And I still get my try at Luke Short?"

"Oh, yes."

"All right, then," Sutherland said. "You got a deal . . . Ed."

# CHAPTER 21

Butler noticed Jerry, the bartender, beckoning him over to the bar.

"What is it?"

"Victor just told me to tell you that Long-haired Jim Courtwright just came in."

"Courtwright," Butler repeated, then said, "Oh, the sheriff?"

"That's right."

"Has he ever come in here before?" Butler asked.

"A few times."

"So? What makes this time different?"

"He asked about you."

Butler looked around.

"Where is he?"

Jerry inclined his head toward the front of the saloon and said, "At the end of the bar, having a free beer."

"Set me up with one down there," Butler said. "I'll talk to him."

Butler walked down the bar until he reached the end, where a tall, slender long-haired man with a badge was nursing a beer. At the same time Jerry arrived with a beer for him.

"Jerry, get the sheriff another one," he said. "That one's getting warm."

"Mr. Butler, I'll bet," Courtwright said.

"You'd win that bet, Sheriff," Butler said. "You a gambling man?"

"No, sir," Courtwright said, "not in the least. It's the reason I keep on tryin' to close down places like this."

"Seems to me your time would be better spent trying to close places like the Bloody Spur."

"Don't you worry," Courtwright said. "I got my sights set on shutting down all of Hell's Half Acre."

Jerry came with the sheriff's fresh beer, but when he tried to remove the half-empty mug left on the bar, the man violently grabbed it and drained it, then gave Jerry back the empty mug.

"What brings you here, Sheriff?" Butler asked.

"I stop in from time to time," the lawman said.

"Yeah, but this time you asked for me."

"Well, I thought I'd just make the acquaintance of the new man in town," Courtwright said. "Lots of card players come in, gamble a few days, and move on. It seems you're stayin' awhile. It would be rude of me not to be hospitable."

"Well, thank you kindly for the welcome," Butler said.

"I also wanted to talk to you about a rumor I heard goin' around."

"Oh? What would that be?"

"A rumor that there's gonna be lots of trouble in some of our town's gambling establishments."

"Trouble?"

"Gunplay, killin', that sort of thing."

"Now, Sheriff, why would that concern you?" Butler asked. "I would think you wouldn't mind some gunplay and killin' between gamblers. Kind of do your job for you."

"Yeah, you'd think that. Wouldn't ya?" Courtwright said. "Except I'm just lookin' to run you fellers out of town, not kill you."

"Well, we appreciate it, Sheriff," Butler said. "Anything else I can do for you?"

"You're a real operator, aintcha?"

"Sorry?"

"You already got yerself situated here at the top gambling house in town," Courtrwright said. "Now, how'd you do that?"

Butler smiled and said, "Charm, Sheriff, pure charm."

# CHAPTER 22

———◆———

Sutherland had no qualms about bushwacking Butler. The fact was, shooting him in the back was the most efficient way of getting rid of him. It would be quick and easy and—he'd get away with it. That was the most important part of the plan.

Now, when it came to killing Luke Short, he would do that one face-to-face. That was the killing where there was a reputation involved. Killing Butler face-to-face would do nothing for his reputation, and it would be taking an unnecessary risk.

That was the reason Sutherland was on the roof of a building across the street from the White Elephant Saloon, with a rifle. From his vantage point he could see both the saloon and Butler's hotel. He was a patient man. He had some beef jerky, a canteen of water, and he could simply piss on the roof if he had to. For anything else he'd just clench his butt cheeks for as long as it took.

And he didn't have to supply a body in order to collect the price on Butler's head. All he had to do was send a telegram, and wait. Once the kill was confirmed, he'd get his money. Whoever the man was who had put the bounty on Butler's head, he had taken every precaution to make sure he was never tied to it, and that the payment would be made.

Sutherland sighted down the barrel of his rifle, picked out a practice target and pretended to pull the trigger. The practice target's head exploded. Sutherland was almost as good with a rifle as he was with a handgun. Taking Luke Short face-to-face with a pistol was going to elevate him to legend status. Taking Butler with a rifle was going to put him on easy street. He had known for years that both of those conditions were in his future. All he had to do was align himself with the right people, and wait.

Ed Cramer was a nobody, the owner of a few pigsty gambling halls he thought made him a businessman and gentleman-gambler. But although he was a nobody, he had led Sutherland to both Butler and Short. And when both of those men were dead and gone, well he'd have no further need of Mr. Cramer.

Would he?

Ed Cramer was waiting for the word from Sutherland that Butler had been taken care of. This man Butler was an unnecessary interruption in Cramer's plan to get rid of Luke Short and, eventually, become the top gambling entrepreneur in Fort Worth, Texas. He'd had Bill Ward and the White Elephant in his sights before Short came along. Once the little dandy was gone, he'd go to work on Ward again, become his partner, then kill him and take over.

But Ed Cramer didn't do his own killing. That was

what he had Sutherland for. To kill Butler, Luke Short, and then, eventually, Bill Ward. And after all the killing was done, Cramer wouldn't need the man anymore, and he'd finally get around to doing his own killing—one killing—himself.

The more Luke Short thought about it, the more convinced he was he should have killed Ed Cramer a long time ago.

Oh, not the day he'd shoved his gun into Cramer's mouth. Much as he would have liked to, there were just too many witnesses that day. That was just fun. No, there had been other times in the past when he might have done it. Maybe, when a time like that came again, he'd seize it and get the man out of his hair.

As he came down the stairs from the casino he saw Butler finishing up his conversation with Jim Courtwright. There was another man he was going to have to kill in the future. He knew it.

As Butler made his way through the room he intercepted him.

"What'd Courtwright want?" he asked.

"He wanted to welcome me to town—"

"That lying sonofa—"

"—and I think he was telling me that he hoped we'd all kill each other."

"All?"

"Us evil gamblers."

"Ah, that sounds more like him."

"What's his beef with gamblers?" Butler asked.

"Don't know," Short said. "Maybe he wants to be one but just can't do it. Maybe he's got religion. Whatever it is, I want him to keep it away from me. I've got enough problems."

"Luke, I want to get something to eat outside of here," Butler said. "You mind?"

"No, go ahead," Short said. "Just remember how quiet it's been, and be careful."

"I'm always careful."

Butler headed for the door.

# CHAPTER 23

When Butler walked through the batwing doors of the White Elephant, Sutherland was ready with his rifle. Butler was in the clear and Sutherland prepared to take his killing shot.

Butler came out the doors, looked both ways, and then headed down the street, away from his hotel and away from the White Elephant.

As Butler went out, Victor glanced through the window. There was just enough sun left for it to glint off something metal on the roof across the street. Victor looked again, saw the man with the rifle and ran for the front doors.

As Victor came out the door shouting, Butler turned quickly. Victor was pointing at something across the street, and then the first shot came. It shattered a window behind Butler as he fell to the ground.

The second shot killed Victor instantly.

Butler dropped as Sutherland shot, causing him to miss and break the window behind Butler. It was that other man's fault—and Sutherland took a bead on him, shooting him through the head. He didn't waste any more shots, just took his rifle and canteen and got out of there.

Luke Short heard the shot, and then the shattering of glass. Customers heard it, too, but they didn't move. The last thing they wanted to do was run outside in the middle of a firefight.

Short, on the other hand, palmed his pistol and ran for the door. As he got outside he almost tripped over Victor's body.

"Damn it!" he swore.

Butler got to his feet and rushed to Victor just as Short came out the door.

"Who'd want to kill Victor?" Short asked.

"He wasn't the target," Butler said. "I was. Victor came out shouting and saved my life. The first shot missed me, and the second got him."

"From where?"

"Across the street, on the roof," Butler said. "I'm sure the shooter is gone now, but I'm going to take a look, anyway."

Finally, someone else came outside. It was Jerry, the bartender.

"Take care of him," Short said. "We'll be back."

"What do I tell the law, boss?" Jerry asked.

"Forget it," Short shouted back as he ran across the street after Butler, "the law will never show up."

\* \* \*

Up on the roof, Short and Butler looked down at the front of the White Elephant.

"Clear shot," Short said, "and a clear view of both your hotel and the saloon. Looks like Cramer's man fired the first shot."

"Not necessarily," Butler said.

"What do you mean?"

"There's something I haven't told you about me, Luke," Butler said.

"You want to share it now?"

Butler nodded, then told Luke Short about the private bounty on his head.

"And you think that's what this was?"

"One of two things: Cramer, or somebody looking for that bounty."

"Or both," Short said. "We know Cramer was going to have you checked out. If someone checked you out real good, Butler, would they come up with that bounty?"

"Probably."

"Then this could be both," Short said. "Whoever Cramer sent after you would not only do the job his boss wanted but collect that bounty, as well."

"Still can't help thinking I got poor Victor killed," Butler said.

"The blame for that goes to the shooter, my friend," Short said, slapping Butler on the shoulder, "not the intended victim."

# CHAPTER 24

Short and Butler walked the length and width of the roof. The only place they found anything was right in front. Scuff marks, a place where a couple of knees had probably spent some time.

"I haven't been on the trail in a while," Short said, "but it looks to me like somebody spent some time here, waiting."

"What are those spots?" Butler asked, pointing.

"Urine," Short said. "That's why I say he was here a while." He bent over, looked at something but didn't touch it. "Here are a couple of pieces of chewed jerky."

"Somebody really put time into this," Butler said.

"And they're not going to be happy they missed you and got the wrong man."

"They'll try again."

"Let's get downstairs, and get you inside," Short said. "Whatever is going on, looks like you're the first target."

As Short had predicted Long-haired Jim Courtwright did not appear. As far as the lawman was concerned, a dead gambler was a good gambler—and that went for people like Victor, who worked for gamblers.

When they got inside they saw that Jerry had gotten help carrying Victor inside.

"Take him to the office," Short said. "We'll have the undertaker pick him up."

"Walk right through the place with him, Luke?" Jerry asked. "It's real busy."

"Who are you kiddin', Jerry," Luke said. "Half of these men won't even notice you."

Jerry signaled the men he'd recruit and together they picked Victor up and carried him to the office. They passed Bill Ward along the way.

"What the hell happened?" he demanded. He was looking at the shattered window.

"Somebody tried to kill Butler," Short said.

"Victor warned me, and got killed for it."

"And the window?"

"The bullet meant for me missed and shattered the window," Butler said. "But I'm fine, thanks for asking."

Ward looked properly chastised.

"I'm sorry Butler," he said. "Of course I'm glad you're all right, and I'm sorry Victor's dead."

"We'll get somebody to fix the window, Bill," Short said. "Don't worry."

"I'm not—"

"What about Victor's family?" Butler asked. "Somebody is going to have to tell them."

"He didn't have any," Short said. "This place is the closest thing he had to a home."

"Look," Ward said, "I didn't mean—"

"We'll be paying for his funeral," Short said, "right, Bill?"

"Yes, of course we will."

Jerry reappeared at that moment.

"Send somebody for the undertaker," Short told him, "and get somebody to board that window up until we can get it fixed."

"Okay, boss."

Short turned to Butler.

"You take your meals inside from now on," Short said. "Also, I'll give you a room upstairs."

"I've got a hotel—"

"I don't care," Short said. "If they want us, next time I want them to have to come in."

"Okay, Luke."

"I'll go with you now to get your gear."

"I don't need a babysitter, Luke," Butler said. "The shooter's gone for now. I'll agree with you wanting me to stay here, but I think I'm safe picking up my things by myself."

"Okay, fine, Short said, "but if you get killed this time it's on your head."

"Should we send for the sheriff?" Ward asked.

"That's a laugh," Short said.

"Why?"

"I'm sure the sheriff has heard all about this by now, Bill," Butler said. "He's hoping one of us is the corpse."

"He's in for a disappointment, then," Short said. "Look, go and get your things before they get a chance to set up again."

"Okay, I'm going," Butler said, "but you've got to do something for me if I stay here."

"What's that?" Short asked.

"Get me a game."

# CHAPTER 25

————◆————

Butler moved his belongings into a room on the second floor of the White Elephant, behind the casino. Luke Short and his wife lived in an apartment down the hall, but she was away and had been since his arrival. It was just as well. Short didn't need to worry about her during the days to come. At least she was safe.

Short led Butler into his rooms for a drink while they discussed what the events of the day meant, and how they should proceed.

"Bill's not going to sit in?" Butler asked.

"I don't know if you've noticed, but Bill's a little slow to act. He doesn't want to get anybody mad at him—which, I think, is one of the main reasons he wanted me as a partner."

"So you could be the bad guy?" Butler asked. "Get people mad at you?"

"Exactly" Short said, "not that I mind, you understand. I'm pretty much at the point in my life when I can't stand most people, anyway. You're a little young for that. Give it ten more years."

Butler doubted that he was ten years younger than

Short. He was also closer than ten years to feeling the way Short felt about people. That tended to happen when so many of them had tried to kill him.

"Luke, I haven't said it yet, but I'm sorry about Victor."

"Yeah," Short said, "he was a good man. You could trust him to do what he could do, you know what I mean?"

"Yes."

"He never disappointed me by trying to do more, and then failing."

"Luke, you got any other men we can count on, or is it just going to be you and me?"

"I told you about the two bartenders. They can fight, and they can fire a shotgun."

"Can they hit anything?"

Short looked away and repeated, "They can fire a shotgun."

"Hard to miss with one of those," Butler said.

"Yeah, well, let's not count on them hitting anything."

"So basically it's you and me."

"Yes," Short said, "but so far only one guy took a shot at you. I think we can handle one guy."

"And how many others do you think Ed Cramer will send after us?" Butler asked.

"I don't know," Short said. "I'm not sure if he wants a war or not."

"A war . . ." Butler said.

That's exactly what Butler ended up involved with in Dodge City, but then he had Jim and Bat Masterson and Neal Brown on his side.

"Maybe it won't be a war," Short said. "Maybe everything will just . . . work out for the best, huh? What do you think of that?"

"And just how would that go?" Butler asked.

"I don't know," Short said. "Maybe, since whoever Cramer sent after you missed, he'll change his mind. He'll know we know he's behind it, and maybe he'll decide to lay low for a while."

"Or maybe," Butler said, "somebody'll just . . . kill him."

"Well," Luke Short said, "wouldn't that be nice of someone, to kill him for us."

Zeke had something stuck in his teeth, which was odd, because he only had some stumps left in his mouth. He'd always thought that the good thing about not having a mouthful of teeth was that nothing would ever get caught, but now he saw that he was wrong.

"Crap," he said.

There were a few customers at the bar, who looked up and stared at him.

"Ah, mind yer business."

He needed a toothpick. He knew his boss kept some on his desk, and he wasn't supposed go in his boss's office, anyway. But it was early in the morning and the boss wouldn't be in yet.

"I'll be right back," he told the man at the bar. They were all regulars, came staggering in as soon as Zeke opened the doors at nine A.M. It was like that in Hell's Half Acre. Nobody cared if a saloon opened early, or if a bunch of men drank in the morning.

Zeke walked to the back, looked around, then pushed aside the curtain and entered. He started for the desk, saw his boss seated there, and stammered, "Hey, uh, boss, I was just—" but then he noticed something.

Ed Cramer's head was splattered all over the wall.

# CHAPTER 26

When Sheriff Jim Courtwright arrived at the White Elephant that afternoon he came with two deputies. They stopped at the bar and he said to Jerry, "Get your boss out here."

"Mr. Ward?"

"You know who I'm talkin' about," Courtwright said. "Luke Short."

"Mr. Short's not here," Jerry said. "If you want to talk to a boss, it's gotta be Mr. Ward."

"All right," Courtwright said. "Bring out Mr. Ward."

"I'll get 'im."

It wasn't three yet, the White Elephant was far from busy. Courtwright was able to watch Jerry the whole way as he walked to the back of the huge room. The bartender knocked on a door, stuck his head in, then out, turned and waved at Courtwright to come ahead. The sheriff crossed the floor with his deputies in tow. When he reached Jerry the barman said, "You can go in."

"Wait out here, boys," he told his deputies, and went inside.

Bill Ward stood up, came around the desk, and asked, "What can I do for you, Sheriff?"

Courtwright ignored Ward's outstretched hand.

"You can tell me where your partner is."

"Luke?"

"You got another partner"

"No, just Luke."

"Of course I'm lookin' for Short," Courtwright said, impatiently. "Where the hell is he?"

"I don't know where Luke is at the moment," Ward said. "Is there something I can do for you?"

"Not if you can't tell me where he is."

"I can tell him you're looking for him."

"Warn him, you mean?"

"About what?" Ward asked. "What's this all about, anyway?"

"You don't know?"

"No, I don't know." Now Ward was starting to get impatient.

"One of your competitors," Courtwright said, "one of your . . . oh hell, Ed Cramer, had the back of his head blown all over his office last night."

"Cramer's dead?"

"That's what usually happens when you put a gun in a man's mouth and pull the trigger."

"What makes you think it was Luke?" Ward asked.

"Well, let's see, I already have witnesses who saw him jam a gun in Ed Cramer's mouth and threaten to use it if he sent anyone here to the White Elephant with . . . let's say, bad intentions?"

"I still don't see—"

"The last I heard somebody shot out one of your windows yesterday," Courtwright added. "Oh, and killed one of your men."

"So, you think Luke went to Cramer to get revenge?" Ward asked.

"Sounds pretty good to me."

"And you're here to arrest Luke?"

"No," Courtwright said, "right now I just wanna talk to him. The arrest will come later—and believe me, it'll be a pleasure."

"Sheriff . . . I don't know what to say . . ."

"If I was you I'd tell me where Short is."

"I honestly don't know, Sheriff."

"Okay, let's try this. Where's your man Butler?" the lawman asked.

"I don't know that, either."

"You don't know where your partner or any of your employees are?"

"I know where Jerry is," Ward said. "He's one of my bartenders. He showed you the way back—"

"I know who Jerry is," Sheriff Courtwright said. "You know, I could toss your ass in jail for not cooperating, Ward."

"I'm cooperating as much as I can, Sheriff," Ward said. "Honest."

"All right," Courtwright said. "You tell Short and Butler to stop by my office as soon as they can. They don't want me to come looking for them again, because next time I'll come to arrest 'em."

"For what?"

"Same thing I'll arrest you for," Courtwright said. "Obstruction. If I have to come back, you're all goin' to jail. You got that?"

"I got it."

"Good," Courtwright said. "You gamblers think you can get away with anything. Well, let me tell you, friend, not in my town."

As Courtwright went out the door Ward fell into his chair and wiped his sweaty face with a handkerchief.

# CHAPTER 27

The back door to the office opened and both Luke Short and Butler entered the room.

"How did you know?" Bill Ward asked, still wiping his face.

"The word is all over Hell's Half Acre that Cramer is dead," Short said. "When I heard about it I knew Courtwright would be out to get me."

"So what are you going to do now?" Ward asked. "Run for it?"

"Hell, no," Short said. "I've got too much invested here to go on the run."

"We'll have to find out who did it," Butler said.

"How are you going to do that?" Ward asked. "You're not detectives."

"I've worn a badge, you know, Bill," Short said. "I think I can pretty much figure out what I have to do to find Cramer's killer."

"Then you better do it quick," Ward said, "because he says he's going to throw all of us in jail."

"He's got no reason to lock up you or Butler," Short said. "He was just trying to scare you."

"Well, he did a damned good job," Ward said. "I've never been in jail."

"You held up really well," Short said. "Thank you."

"Never mind thanking me," Ward said. "Just go out there and find yourself a killer."

"Bill, for a while I'm not going to tell you where I am so when you tell Courtwright, you'll be tellin' him the truth."

"Fine," Ward said. "It was all I could do not to tell him you were right out back."

"Again," Short said, "you did great." He looked at Butler. "We better get out of here."

As they headed for the door that led to the saloon Bill Ward said, "Luke?"

"Yeah, Bill?"

"You didn't, uh, kill Cramer, did you?" Ward asked, stammering a bit.

Short turned to face his partner.

"No, Bill," he said, "I did not kill Cramer."

"Okay," Ward said. "I'm, uh, real sorry I had to ask."

"Yes, Bill," Short said, "so am I."

Short stopped when they stepped out into the saloon, as if he expected to find the sheriff there waiting for him.

"What is it?" Butler asked.

"Nothing."

"What do we do first to find this killer, Luke?" Butler asked.

"We have to go downtown," Short said, "to Hell's Half Acre and start askin' questions."

"That's going to raise a red flag," Butler said. "Word will get around that we're there."

"I know."

"So that's what you want?" Butler said. "When the killer hears we're looking for him he'll come after us."

"Me," Short said, "he'll come lookin' for me."

"What're you—I'm not staying behind, Luke. You hired me to watch your back—"

"You're fired."

"It doesn't matter," Butler said. "I'll follow you there, anyway."

"You're serious."

"Yes."

"Why? You don't owe me anything. And somebody's already tried to kill you. The best thing for you to do is move on, Butler."

"I can't do that, Luke."

"Why not?"

"How would I ever face Bat and Wyatt if I let you get killed?"

They planned to go downtown together, but not travel side by side.

"Just stay behind me, watch my back, and maybe that way we can get the drop on the killer."

"Or whoever he sends against us."

"Cramer didn't treat women very well. No one really mattered to him. Maybe the killer is a woman."

"That's interesting," Butler said. "Maybe his murder had nothing to do with you, or the White Elephant."

"Well, that would be preferable," Short said. "I'd like to keep Bill Ward out of it, if I can."

They stepped out on the street cautiously, looking for gunmen or lawmen.

"Looks like the coast is clear," Short said. "Let's start now and take separate cabs. Once we're down there you can follow on foot at a good distance."

"What about when you go inside to ask questions?"

"You'll have to watch from the window," Short said, "or come in and have a drink."

"Remember," Butler said, "you told me to watch what I drank down there."

"Yeah, well," Short said, patting Butler on the arm, "I guess certain sacrifices will have to be made."

## CHAPTER 28

———◆———

When Luke Short entered the Bloody Spur the bartender, Zeke, went for the shotgun he kept under the bar. Short drew his gun and pointed it at him.

"Don't be stupid," he said.

Zeke froze. There were a few men in the place—two at tables, one standing at the bar—who looked but didn't move.

"You gonna kill me, too?" Zeke asked.

"I'm not going to kill you, too, because I didn't kill your boss."

"Yeah, right," Zeke said. "You said you were gonna blow out the back of his head, and you did."

Short approached the bar and said, "Somebody did. Somebody who knew that killin' him that way would lead to me. Now my question to you is, who did you tell?"

"Me?" Zeke said, staring down the barrel of Short's gun. "I didn't tell nobody. There was plenty of other fellas in here that day, maybe one of them did it."

"Well, that's possible," Short agreed. He turned to

look at the other three men in the place, who immediately turned away.

"Okay, let's try somethin' else," he said to Zeke. "Who found your boss dead?"

"I did."

"Tell me about it."

"It was early—uh, early for him to be in his office. I went in, figuring he wasn't there, and I found him."

"With the back of his head missin'."

Zeke nodded.

"Who else could have had a motive to shoot him?"

"You kiddin'?" Zeke asked. "Anybody down here."

"He wasn't well liked?"

"Nobody's well liked down here," Zeke said. "Everybody's out for themselves."

"So you can't give me a name or two—your boss's biggest enemies?"

"There are other saloons right on this street," Zeke said. "Start with them."

"What about women?"

"He had lots of 'em."

"Did he treat them badly?"

"Well, yeah," Zeke said, as if that was obvious.

"Would any of them have killed him that way?"

"No."

"Why not?"

"Because the kind of woman he kept company with liked bein' treated that way."

Short studied the man for a moment, then decided he was telling the truth. Apparently, when it came to women, Cramer kept to his own kind.

He turned to leave, then thought of something else.

Butler stood outside the Bloody Spur, watching the action from the window. He also had to keep an eye on the street for an ambush, or for the law. He checked out the rooftops across the street, saw a white curtain in a window move. He stared into the window of the Spur again, but this time he was using the reflection. Sure enough, as soon as he looked away the curtain was pushed aside and someone looked out the window again. He didn't see a gun barrel come out. Somebody was just watching him, or watching the Bloody Spur.

Interesting.

"Who was your boss using for bushwacking people?" Short asked Zeke.

"Huh?"

"Come on," Short said, "Cramer had people killed. Who was he usin'? Give me a name."

"I can't do that."

"Why not?"

"H-he'll kill me."

"Who?"

"Sutherlan—" Zeke stopped, as he realized he'd been tricked.

"Finish the name."

"That's it," Zeke said. "Sutherland."

"No first name?"

"If he's got one I don't know it."

"He's a killer?

"I ain't never seen him kill nobody," Zeke said, "but that's his rep."

"And he came in here to see your boss?"

"All the time."

"So maybe he killed him."

"Why would he?" Zeke asked. "The boss paid him."

"Maybe," Short said, "he wasn't payin' him enough anymore."

# CHAPTER 29

Outside Short was surprised to find Butler approaching him.

"You're followin' a little too close, don't you think?" he asked.

"I don't think it matters," Butler said. "There's a window across the street with somebody in it. No gun," he added, to keep Short from dropping to the ground. "Just nosy, I think."

"And?"

"If they make a habit of watching this street, or this saloon, maybe they saw something."

"That means if they're nosy enough," Short said, "they could see what goes on here mornin', noon, and night."

"Now you've got it."

"You know what floor? What door we knock on?"

"I can guess," Butler said, "but I don't want to make it too obvious that we're going over there."

"Okay," Short said, "we'll take a short walk down the block, and then double back across the street."

Butler nodded.

*   *   *

Mary Cronin had lived on Rusk Street for the past twenty years. She'd seen saloons go up and come down and go up again. She'd seen men lie, cheat, steal and kill, and all from her window. Now she was seventy years old and she still prided herself on her eyesight. She lived on money she got from her son every month, cooked all her own food, never left her rooms, and spent most of her waking hours at her window.

As far as she was concerned, this block belonged to her.

When a knock came at her door she was surprised. Nobody ever came to see her but her son, and he had his own key.

She was loath to leave her window—something might happen that she'd miss—but her curiosity got the better of her. Now who could possibly be knocking at her door, and why?

She walked to it, and turned the knob.

Butler had guessed wrong with the first door they knocked on, and they'd interrupted a couple having sex, who acted like they'd been caught doing something wrong. When they realized that the woman's husband had not sent Butler and Short, they cursed them out and slammed the door.

"I get the feeling those people are not married to each other," Short commented.

Shaking his head, Butler led Short to the next door on that floor.

"I hope this is the right one."

Butler knocked. He was about to knock again when the door was opened by an elderly woman.

"Yes?"

"Ma'am," Butler said. "I believe your front window overlooks the street. Am I right?"

The woman frowned, narrowed her eyes.

"Who are you—wait. I know you. You're the two fellas who were just across the street at the Bloody Spur, ain'tcha?"

"Yes, Ma'am, we are," Butler said. "May we come in and talk to you?"

"Is this about the murder?" she asked.

"Yes, Ma'am, it is," Luke Short said.

She looked at his silk hat—which was in his hand—and his walking stick and said, "You're a bit of a dandy, ain'tcha?"

"Yes, Ma'am, I guess I am."

"And you're handsome," she said to Butler.

"Thank you, Ma'am."

"Been a while since I had a handsome man or a dandy call on me," she said. "Now I got one of each. Well, come on in, then. I reckon we got a lot to talk about."

"Thank you, Ma'am," Butler said, as he and Short entered.

Butler walked right to the front window and looked out. He could see the front of the Bloody Spur very clearly. He looked at Short and nodded.

"You young fellas will have tea with me, won'tcha?" the lady asked.

"Ma'am," Luke Short said, "I don't think we have the time—"

"If you wanna know what I know," she said, "you'll make the time."

"And what do you know, Ma'am?" Butler asked.

"I know I ain't had any company for tea in a month of Sundays," she said.

"Ma'am," Butler said, "we'd be delighted to join you for tea."

# CHAPTER 30

———◦◦◦———

They each had a cup of tea and some cookies the woman said she had just made for herself. They found out that her name was Mary Cronin and she had lived there for a very long time.

"I remember when the Bloody Spur went up," she said, "and then all them others followed. I remember when this wasn't called Hell's Half Acre, or the Bloody Third Ward. I remember when decent folks lived here. Now look what we got. Drunks and gamblers." She peered at Butler. "Which one are you?"

He smiled.

"Ma'am, I believe I've been one or the other at certain times of my life."

"Well," she said, "I'm impressed. I do believe that was an honest answer."

"Ma'am," Butler said, "we'd like to ask you about the murder of Ed Cramer. Do you know who Mr. Cramer was?"

"'Course I do, young man. I'm old, I ain't stupid."

"I didn't mean to say that you were, Ma'am—"

"Could you just call me Mary and stop with the Ma'am all the time?"

"I believe I can do that, Mary."

She looked at Short.

"You ever been drunk?"

"I've turned a card and been drunk plenty of times, Mary," Short admitted. "Too many from my wife's point of view."

"Another honest man," Mary said. "I don't know what to do with all this honesty."

"I'll give you some more, then, Mary," Butler said. "My friend Luke, here, has been accused of murdering Ed Cramer. Now, he didn't do it—"

"I know he didn't do it," she said, looking at Short. "You Luke Short?"

"Yes, Ma—Mary."

"I thought so. You had cause to kill Cramer, didn't ya?"

"I did."

"But you didn't do it."

"No."

"I ain't askin' ya," she snapped, "I'm tellin' ya."

"Can you also tell us how you know Luke didn't do it, Mary?"

"Of course I can." She smiled, showing a few gaps where teeth used to be, but the ones she had left looked good and strong. "Because I know who did."

More tea, more cookies, stories about her three husbands, only one of the no-good sonsofbitches gave her a son who was taking care of her.

"Only one son?" Butler asked. "Or only one worth mentioning?"

Short looked at him like he was mad. What did they care about these stories?

"That's a good question, Mr. Butler."

"Just Butler, Ma'am."

"Ain't that a good question, Mr. Short?"

Butler gave Short a look.

"It's Luke, Mary," he said. "Just call me Luke."

"Don't you think Butler's question was a good one?" she pressed on.

"I think it was mighty fine, yes."

She looked at Butler.

"I'll tell ya, I got only one son, but he's takin' real good care of me."

"That's good," he said. "It's important to have a good son."

"What about you?" she asked Butler.

"What about me?"

"Are you a good son to your Ma?"

"I like to think I was."

"Was?"

"She's dead, Mary," he said, then added, "somebody killed her."

"Who?" she asked. "Who killed her?"

"Same people that killed my Pa," Butler said. "I don't know who they are yet, though."

"Yet? You gonna find them?"

"Someday," he said. "Someday I'll find them and kill them all."

She stared at him, then smiled and said, "See that? You are a good son."

She looked at Short, who was hoping she wouldn't ask him about his mother.

"Who thinks you killed Cramer?"

"The sheriff."

"That skunk Courtwright?" she asked,

"I see we agree on somethin', Mary," Short said.

"We agree on more than that, Luke," she said. "We agree that you didn't kill that sonofabitch Cramer."

"But you know who did?" he asked.

"Ya darn tootin' I do."

"And you're gonna tell us?"

She nodded sagely, and said, "I'm gonna tell ya."

# CHAPTER 31

Butler and Short actually walked out of Hell's Half Acre, and then stopped in a small saloon to discuss what they'd found out. They figured it was fairly safe to have a drink there, and each ordered a cold beer.

"I don't know how much good that did," Short admitted. "She saw a man go in, saw a man come out, doesn't know who he was, but had seen him many times before, at odd hours."

"The odd hours part indicates to me that he was doing specialized work for Cramer."

"You mean like killing for him?" Short asked.

"Right."

"And then they had a fallin' out and the employee killed the employer."

"Why not?"

"So what does the killer do now?" Short asked. "He's cut off his source of income."

"There's still the price on my head," Butler said. "It's large enough to make up for losing his employer, until he finds a new one."

"Or," Short said, "maybe he intends to take over Cramer's business."

"If that's the case," Butler said, "then we already have his attention."

"If I stay out in the open to give him a try," Short said, "the sheriff might end up bagging me first."

"Well then, maybe we should just keep walking up and down Rusk Street until he tries for you—or me."

"It ain't natural for a man to have a bull's-eye on his back."

"Tell me about it."

"Sorry," Short said, "I forgot."

"It doesn't matter," Butler said. "I've learned to live with it."

"How do you live with that?"

"How do you, Bat, or Wyatt live with the fact that someone, somewhere, is going to make a try for your reputation?"

"You have a point there," Short said.

They finished their beers and went out onto the street.

"So, do we walk back in?" Butler asked.

Short was considering the question when several men came running at them, from both sides, brandishing guns. Neither man had a chance to draw their own weapon.

"What the hell—" Short said, and then he saw Jim Courtwright coming across the street with a satisfied look on his face.

"Short," the lawman said. "You think I don't have

eyes in the Acre? I knew the minute you and your buddy, here, showed up."

"What do you want, Courtwright?" Short asked, trying to brazen it out. "We've got business—"

"No, no, you have no business today with anybody but me. I'm takin' you in."

"For what?"

"Questioning," Courtwright said. "We're gonna have a nice talk about who killed Ed Cramer—although I think we both know who did it."

"Butler," Short said, "why don't you go back to the White Elephant and tell Bill what's—"

"Oh, no," Courtwright said, "Mr. Butler is gonna come with us. I've got some questions for him, too. Now raise your hands up so my boys can take your guns."

Butler and Short complied.

"Now we'll all take a nice ride to my office," Courtwright said. "We have lots to talk about . . ."

When they got to the sheriff's office, Butler and Short were put in cells next to each other and left there for an hour or so. Finally, Courtwright came in with two deputies, who opened their cell doors.

"Okay, you two, out," Courtwright said.

"Finally came to your senses, huh?" Short asked. "I won't press charges for false arrest—"

"Shut up, Short," Courtwright said. "I got enough to arrest you right now, and that's what I'm doin'."

"What, no talk?" Butler asked.

"You shut your mouth or I'll arrest you, too."

"You mean you're not?"

"You're free to go," Courtwright said. "Take my advice and keep goin'."

They walked Short and Butler out into the office, where Short got pushed into a chair. Butler was given back his gun, unloaded. Yeah, he thought, as if he'd try to shoot his way out with Short.

"Like I said," Courtwright said to Butler, "there's the door. Just keep goin', friend."

"I'll see you soon, Luke," Butler said. "Don't worry about a thing."

"See you, Butler," Short said.

"If anything happens to him while he's in your custody," Butler said, "you'll answer to me."

Courtwright snarled, "Get out!"

# CHAPTER 32

When Al Newman opened the door to his home and saw Butler standing on the doorstep he was pleasantly surprised.

"Got a game?" he asked.

"I've got a big game," Butler said, "and you're going to be one of the main players."

"Come on in," Newman said, "and tell me all about it. I've got the feeling we're not talking about poker."

Butler had returned to the White Elephant, found Jerry, and told him what had happened. He then asked the bartender if he knew where Al Newman lived.

"What do you want with him?"

"He's a lawyer."

"Ain't he supposed to be retired?"

"Maybe I'll bring him out of retirement," Butler said. "Do you know where he lives?"

"No," Jerry said, "but try Mr. Ward. They're supposed to be friends."

That was right. Butler remember Newman saying he

was friends with Ward, which was not enough to get him into Luke Short's game.

"Where is he?"

"In the office."

Butler walked in without knocking, surprising Ward.

"What the—"

"Luke's been arrested for the murder of Ed Cramer," Butler said.

"How did that happen?" Ward demanded. "I thought you two were going to lay low?"

"It doesn't matter how it happened, just that it did," Butler said. "Luke's going to need a lawyer. Do you know where Al Newman lives?"

"Well, yes, but Al's retired—"

"I don't care," Butler said. "I'm going to ask him to represent Luke, try to get him out of Courtwright's custody before something happens."

"You don't think that Courtwright would—" Ward started, but Butler cut him off.

"I don't know what can happen in that jail," he said. "Anything's possible. Come on, Bill, give me the address."

Ward gave Butler the address and Butler immediately went to the man's house.

As Butler followed Newman to the living room a woman came out of the kitchen, drying her hands on the apron she wore around her waist.

"I thought I heard a knock—oh, we have company."

"Helen, this is Mr. Butler," Newman said. "I told you about him."

"Oh, yes," she said, with a smile, "this is the gentleman who got you into an all-night poker game at the White Elephant." The handsome woman in her late forties looked Butler up and down, then said, "I'm sorry I can't say it's nice to meet you, Mr. Butler. I really don't think my husband should be patronizing places like that." She looked at her husband. "I have a roast in the oven." She turned and went back into the kitchen.

"That was rude," Newman said. "I apologize; I'll have a talk with her."

"That's okay," Butler said. "I think she'll probably be even madder at me when she finds out why I'm here."

"And just why are you here?"

"Jim Courtwright has arrested Luke Short for murdering Ed Cramer."

"Cramer? The owner of the Bloody Spur?"

"That's him."

Newman rubbed his jaw with his right hand.

"Did he do it?"

"No, he didn't do it," Butler said. "I want you to get him out."

"Me?" Newman said. "I told you the other night, Butler, I'm retired. I can recommend somebody, but that's all I can—"

"That'll take too long," Butler said. "Courtwright hates Luke, Al. Something bad will happen if we leave him in that jail."

"What kind of evidence does Courtwright have?" Newman asked.

"None, because Luke didn't do it. Oh, he's got a witness who saw Luke threaten to blow the back of Cramer's head out."

"And is that how he died?"

"Yes."

Newman turned and looked over his shoulder at the kitchen.

"I have to talk to my wife," he said. "Wait for me out front."

"What if she says no?" Butler asked.

"You misunderstand me," Newman said. "I'm not asking her permission, I'm just going to talk to her. Wait outside."

# CHAPTER 33

Al Newman came walking out of the courthouse with Luke Short at his side.

"You did it!" Butler said. "You got him out."

"The judge I spoke to did not take kindly to Sheriff Courtwright's preemptive action," Newman said. "He told the sheriff to make sure he had some evidence next time he made an arrest."

Butler shook Short's hand.

"He also told me to watch my ass," Short said. "The judge is among those in our fair city in favor of closing down the gambling houses."

"And he still cut you loose," Butler said. "Sounds like a fair-minded man."

"He is," Newman said. "It's the only reason Short is out."

"No, it's not," Short said to Newman. "I'm out because you vouched for me. I owe you big, Al."

"Just remember that next time you're putting together a big game," Newman said.

"Don't worry, I will."

Short stepped into the street to stop a passing cab. Newman grabbed Butler's shoulder.

"I did this as a favor to you, you know," he said. "You're the one who got me into that game the other night, not Luke."

"I don't care why you did it, Al," Butler said, "just that you did it." He shook the man's hand. "Thank you. And tell your wife I'm sorry."

"It won't do any good," Newman said. "The only person she's mad at more than you is me."

Newman pointed at Short, who was holding a cab for Butler.

"Keep him out of trouble."

"Al, the only way we're going to clear him is to find out who really did it," Butler said, "and we have an idea. We talked to this woman—"

Newman put both hands up, palms out, and said, "I don't want to hear it. Just keep in mind that I vouched for Luke."

"I will," Butler said. "Thanks again."

Butler joined Short in the cab as Newman walked the other way.

"Worried about his reputation?" Short asked.

"He did put it on the line for you," Butler pointed out.

"I get the feeling he did it for you," Short said, "but whatever the reason, I'm thankful. I think Courtwright was planning on having me killed while trying to escape tonight."

"That's why I knew we had to get you out of there fast," Butler said.

"Well, I appreciate the quick action, Butler, but we still have to find the man old Mary Cronin saw coming and going in and out of the Bloody Spur."

"Sutherland," Butler said.

"That's what the bartender said. So our job right now is to find a man named Sutherland."

"Who may or may not have a reputation as a killer," Butler said.

"My thinkin' is," Short said, "this is a man who's still lookin' for a reputation."

"So he can kill you and get himself known, and then kill me and get himself some money."

"And after all that," Short said, "maybe he can take over Cramer's businesses."

"Not if we can help it."

When they got back to the White Elephant, Short went to the office to talk to his partner. He told Butler he was going to have to calm Bill Ward down and it would probably take a while.

"I'm afraid he's either going to have a heart attack," Short said, "or offer to buy me out."

"Without you he'd lose the gambling business you bring in," Butler said.

"That may not be worth it for him," Short said, "if I keep finding trouble."

"What happens if it's trouble that keeps finding you?" Butler asked.

"I don't think he'll see the difference," Short said. "I'll see you later on. Thanks again."

"Glad I could help."

"So far," Short said, "I can honestly report to Bat and Wyatt that you've been doing a bang-up job of keeping me out of jail . . . and alive."

"I'll see if I can keep to that high standard," Butler said.

# CHAPTER 34

Butler had never heard the name Sutherland before today. More importantly Luke Short, who knew everybody there was to know who had a reputation with cards or a gun, had never heard the name. Short was probably right. This was a local tough looking to make a name for himself. And if he was local, he had to be known by locals.

Butler knew the men he'd played poker with, and the only local there had been Al Newman. He couldn't go to him for help, anymore, without risking the great wrath of his wife.

He'd known Victor somewhat, but Victor was dead.

That left the bartender Jerry, who Luke Short seemed to think of as a scrapper.

As usual, Jerry was behind the bar. In fact, Butler couldn't recall a time when Jerry wasn't working behind the bar. The man never seemed to take any time off. But he was a local, so Butler decided to try the name on him.

He elbowed his way to the bar. Men moved aside because if they didn't know him by name, they knew him on sight as somebody who was close to Luke Short.

He got Jerry's attention and waved him over. When the bartender pointed to the beer questioningly, Butler shook his head and waved him over again.

"What's the deal" Jerry asked. "Not thirsty today?"

"How long have you lived in Fort Worth?" Butler asked him.

"All my life," Jerry said. "Why?"

"Do you know a man named Sutherland?"

Butler saw the man stiffen, knew immediately that he recognized the name. Now the question came up, was he going to lie about it?

"Why are you askin' about him?"

"Because I need to find him."

"You don't want to find him, Butl—"

"Look," Butler said, "I'm pretty sure he killed Victor, and tried to kill me. I also think he killed Ed Cramer. So if you know anything about him, now's the time to spill it. Luke's life is on the line here, too."

"Mr. Short? Why?"

"Because the law thinks he killed Cramer. Come on, Jerry. We need your help here."

"Look, all I know is that he hangs out downtown," Jerry said.

"In Hell's Half Acre?"

"Well . . . sort of."

"What does that mean, Jerry?"

"I'm a bartender, I hear talk—but that's all it is, talk. I don't know nothin' for sure."

"So tell me what you don't know for sure," Butler said, "and I'll check it out."

"There's a whorehouse on Main Street, just a couple of blocks off the docks. He's supposed to be there a lot."

"Tell me more."

"I don't know no more," Jerry said. "There's supposed to be a girl there he likes."

"Come up with a name."

"Geez, Butler, you want—wait a minute," Jerry said. "I remember. Somebody said it was Lily, like that actress, Lilly Langtry."

"Lily."

"That's all I know," Jerry said, "I swear. Butler, if I could help Mr. Short I would."

"I believe you, Jerry," Butler said. "Thanks for the information. Now one more thing."

"What's that?"

"If Luke asks you where I am, you don't know."

"Okay."

"And don't tell him what you told me."

"You ain't goin' into Hell's Half Acre alone, are you, Butler?"

"Just remember," Butler said. "Don't tell him about Sutherland."

"Nothin'."

"Nothing."

"You want me to lie to Mr.—"

"I don't want him going down there, Jerry," Butler said. "The sheriff already has it in for him, and Sutherland likes to shoot people from rooftops. I want Luke to stay inside, where it's safe."

Jerry looked confused, but he said, "Well, all right, if that's the way you want it."

"That's how I want it."

"What about Mr. Ward?" Jerry said. "What if he asks where you are?"

"He won't," Butler said, "but if he does, don't tell him, either."

"So nobody but me is gonna know you're down there?"

"Now you've got it," Butler said. "Thanks, Jerry."

Jerry watched as Butler went out the door. He didn't like the responsibility he'd just been given.

# CHAPTER 35

———◆◆◆———

Butler went up to his room and changed from his usual suit to trail clothes he thought would help him blend in more down in the Acre. Then he carefully left the White Elephant by the back way because he didn't want to run into Short.

He got a cab down to Rusk Street, then decided to walk from there. He took a quick look in the window of the Bloody Spur, saw business as usual. Zeke was behind the bar, and there were only a few men around. He looked at the building across the street, saw Mary Cronin at her window, but she didn't wave. She didn't recognize him, which was fine with him.

He thought about going inside to talk to Zeke, but he thought Short had gotten all there was to get out of the man—except for who was running the place now. Still, if he went inside to ask, word would get around and that would defeat the purpose of wearing his trail clothes.

He moved on.

He figured he must have missed the whorehouse he was looking for, so he kept going until he got to the docks, then retraced his steps. He found himself walking along with a group of dock workers who had apparently just gotten off work. He decided to cross the street and follow them discreetly. He bet that at least one of them would lead him to Lily.

Several of them went to saloons, others to a small restaurant, and he was sure some of them went home. Two of them, however, led him to a two-story structure that looked as if it had once been a hotel. They were laughing and slapping each other on the back as they went in.

Butler waited, and sure enough several more men appeared and entered, in the same jovial mood. Finally, he crossed the street, hoping he wouldn't need some sort of code word to get in.

There were no markings on the building to indicate what kind of business it housed. Butler didn't know what the law was in Fort Worth when it came to prostitution.

He mounted the three steps and knocked on the door. A small slot in the door slid open. He found himself looking into a pair of brown eyes with dark eyebrows.

"Can I help you?" a man's voice asked.

"I'd, uh, like to come in."

"For what?"

"Um . . ."

"Do you know what kind of a business we run here?" the voice asked.

"Well, of course. This is a . . . bordello."

"No," the voice said, "this is a whorehouse. I'm afraid I'm not going to let you in unless you can tell us who sent you?"

"I'd like to see Lily."

"Lots of men want to see Lily," the man said, "and Angie, and Dina, and Babe—"

"Babe?"

"Hey, it's her name."

"Okay," Butler said, "sorry." If he didn't think of something fast he wasn't going to get inside.

"So, if you don't got a name for me you're gonna have to move—"

"Sutherland."

"What?"

"Sutherland told me to come," Butler said.

"Did he tell you to ask for Lily?"

This sounded like a trick question. He thought a moment before coming up with what he thought was a likely answer.

"No," he said, "as a matter of fact he said when I came here I should stay away from her."

Suddenly, he heard the lock on the door and it opened, revealing a sticky man in his forties standing there. He recognized him by his eyebrows.

"That's Sutherland," he said. "If he scared off a few more customers, Lily would have to start waitin' tables some place. Come on in, friend. Welcome to Rosie's."

Butler entered, the man closed the door behind them, and locked it.

"Go on into the sitting room," the man said. "Rosie and the girls are there."

"Thanks."

Butler went through a doorway and found himself in the sitting room with more than half a dozen girls. The furnishings were gold and maroon. A woman in her fifties, wearing a dress that matched the furnishings, approached him with a wide smile and deep, powdered, slightly wrinkled cleavage.

"Welcome to Rosie's, friend," she said. She placed her hands on her hips and took a step back, looking him up and down. "You're a handsome one. My girls are gonna like you. Come on and take your pick—or maybe I should just let them bid on you."

# CHAPTER 36

Butler understood why he saw so many men coming into this place. He was expecting some suspect-looking whores, at best, but every girl in the room—except for Madame Rosie—was beautiful.

"Would you like a drink while you're tryin' to decide?" Rosie asked. "You can have beer, whiskey, coffee . . . how about some music? Our piano player can play anything you like."

He needed to stall.

"I think I'll have a beer," he said, "but no music. I'd like to talk to these fine ladies."

"Well, talk away, friend," Rosie said. "Talkin' is free here at Rosie's. Have a seat somewhere and we'll get you that beer."

There were several girls seated on a large sofa and they scooted either way to allow him to sit in between. Once he was down, he found himself pressed between some prime, sweet-smelling female flesh.

He had to force himself to remember he was not there for pleasure.

\* \* \*

The man who answered the door went up the back stairs to the second floor, walked quickly down the hall. He knocked on the door of room 5—Lily's room.

"What?" Lily shouted.

"Sutherland," the man said, "it's Walt, from downstairs."

"Go away," Sutherland's voice came.

"It's important," Walt said. He waited, then added, "You told me to let you know if anybody asked for you."

Seconds later the door opened and Sutherland appeared, holding a sheet around his waist. Since he had the sheet, Lily was left on the bed, nude.

"Somebody asked for me?"

"A fella came to the door, gave your name in order to get in," Walt said.

"And you let him in?"

"I didn't know I wasn't supposed to."

"Where is he?"

"In the parlor with the girls."

"What's he doin'?"

"I don't know, pickin', I guess."

"Okay."

"What're you gonna do?"

"None of your business," Sutherland snapped. "Go back where you belong."

He slammed the door, turned to face Lily. She was a tall, busty brunette who had convinced Sutherland he was the best man she'd ever been to bed with. Of course, she'd convinced a lot of other men of the same thing. The only difference was, Sutherland knew she was lying, but he didn't care.

"Comin' back to bed, sweetie?"

"Afraid not," Sutherland said. "I've got to get dressed."

If it was a lawman downstairs, he didn't want to get in a shootout with him. If it was Luke Short or Butler, this wasn't the place to face them.

"Does this place have a back way?" he asked Lily.

"I think it's blocked."

He pulled on his pants, and then his boots. When he strapped on his gun, he walked to the window and looked out. He was on the second floor, but it wasn't a long drop. He was a tall man and figured it shouldn't be too bad.

"Are you goin' out the window?" Lily asked.

"There's somebody downstairs I'm not ready to see," he said.

"Well, I hope you were intendin' to pay before you leave," Lily said. "Rosie don't like to be stiffed."

Hurriedly, Sutherland took some money from his pocket and dropped it on the dresser, then opened the window and climbed out. He dangled there for a moment, then dropped. The landing jarred him, but didn't break or sprain anything.

He was in the alley next to the building. He moved to a window he knew looked in on the parlor. The drapes were parted just enough for him to see Butler on the sofa with some of the girls. They had him tangled up good in their arms and legs. For a moment he considered busting in and taking him, but there was too much that could go wrong in a room full of people.

He hated not taking a shot when he was so close, but he was more concerned at that moment with how Butler had found him. If the gambler could do it, so could the sheriff.

He decided to go back to the Bloody Spur and have a little chat with Zeke.

# CHAPTER 37

———◆———

By chatting with the girls, Butler was able to determine that Lily was not in the parlor with them. With just a little more encouragement one of the girls said Lily was upstairs with her best customer.

"Not her favorite customer," one of the other girls was quick to point out, "but her best."

She was a blonde named Kimmie, while the girl on his left was a redhead named Ruby.

"Oh," Butler said, "that would probably be my friend Sutherland."

"You know Sutherland?" Ruby asked.

"You're friends with him?" Kimmie asked, clearly disappointed.

"Well," Butler said, "not exactly friends. I've just heard him talk about this place, and Lily."

"Lily's not so special," Ruby said, sniffing.

"You'd be a lot better off with one of us," Kimmie said, stroking his right thigh.

"That's the truth," Ruby said, stroking his left.

Butler felt he had two ways to go. Take one of the

girls upstairs and try to find Sutherland, or wait outside for the man to leave.

"So, do you girls have a price for all night?" he asked.

"Oh, Rosie don't like a man to stay all night," Ruby said. "She says we can make more money with more men."

"I see."

Both girl's hands were becoming insistent, so he sprang to his feet.

"I guess I'll come back, then."

"When?" Ruby asked, with big cow eyes, which meant to make her look disappointed.

"Why?" Kimmie asked. "For Lily?"

"No," he said, "I have to decide between the two of you, and I can't make that decision now. It's just too hard."

Coyly, Ruby said, "You could take us both."

"Oh God," he said, clutching his chest, "I think that would give me a heart attack. No, I think I'll make my decision and then come back."

"If you go red, you won't go back," Ruby said.

"That don't even rhyme," Kimmie told her.

"I don't care—"

"I'll see you girls soon."

He had to get past Rosie on the way to the door. She couldn't believe he was leaving.

"You can take your time and decide here," she told him.

"Too much pressure," he said. "Don't worry. I'll be back."

He hurriedly went out the door, despite her protests. The same man opened it to let him out, and he got a bad feeling from him.

"What's your name?" he asked.

"Walt." The man's eyes slid away.

"Okay, Walt, thanks."

"Sure."

Butler left. It was getting dark by this time. He decided to look for a likely place to stand and watch and wait. First, he checked out the alley next to the building, but that was no good. He finally decided on a doorway across the street.

He watched as men who had gone in before him came out, and still no Sutherland. More and more he had a bad feeling about the door man, Walt. Lo and behold, while he was thinking of him, the man appeared at the door. Apparently, he was through for the day. Walt stepped down, looked both ways, and began to walk in a direction that took him away from the docks.

Butler quickly crossed the street. Instead of simply intercepting the man he slammed into him and pulled him into a wall.

"Hey, wha—"

"Hello, Walt," Butler said.

"Who are y— Hey? What're ya doin'?"

"Sutherland was upstairs the whole time, wasn't he?" Butler asked. "You went up and told him I was looking for him. What'd he do, go out a back door? Or a window?"

"Hey, I don't know—"

"Yeah, you do." Butler pulled him away from the

wall, then slammed him back into it. The man tried to get away, but he was smaller and Butler was stronger.

"All you've got to do is tell me the truth, Walt," Butler said.

"H-he'll kill me."

Butler took his gun out and pressed it to the side of Walt's head.

"Why don't I just kill you now, and get it over with?" he suggested.

"No, no!" Walt said. "Wait. Yeah, okay, he was upstairs with Lily. I—I tipped him off that you was downstairs."

"He go out the back?"

"The back door's sealed," Walt said. "He musta gone out a window down to the alley."

"Can you see the parlor from the alley?"

"Yeah, yeah, I think you can."

So all Sutherland had to do was look in the window to see him. Apparently, he wasn't prepared to take another try at killing him.

"Okay," Butler said, "one more question. Where does Sutherland live?"

"Wha— you crazy? I dunno that."

"Then where would he go?"

"Anywhere," Walt said. "Anywhere in Hell's Half Acre. This is where he feels at home."

Butler thought a moment. Sutherland was going to be wondering how Butler found him. Where would he go to find the answer?

Butler released Walt.

"Okay," he said. "Get going."

"You ain't gonna kill me?"

"Not even going to put a scratch on you," Butler said. "Get out of here!"

Walt skulked away and Butler was sure he'd tell Sutherland about this.

He was counting on it.

# CHAPTER 38

When Sutherland entered the Bloody Spur his anger was so apparent that Zeke—not even knowing if it was meant for him—ran out from behind the bar and bolted toward the back of the room.

Sutherland caught him in a few steps. The three or four customers who were there watched as he grabbed the back of his collar and walked him through the curtains into what used to be Ed Cramer's office. There was still dried blood and bits of brain on the wall behind the desk.

"Wait, wait, wait—" Zeke was shouting.

"Sit down!"

Sutherland slammed him into his boss's old chair, also covered with dried blood.

"Oh, no, no," Zeke said, trying to get up, but Sutherland drew his gun and pointed it at his face. The bartender stopped struggling and stared at the gun with wide, frightened eyes.

"You told Butler about Rosie's, didn't you?" Sutherland demanded.

"No, I didn't," Zeke said. "How was I supposed to know about Rosie's? I didn't know you was there."

"You know about Rosie's, and you know about Lily," Sutherland said. "If you didn't tell him, who did?"

"I dunno," Zeke said. "Hey, come on, Sutherland. You know me."

"Yeah, Zeke, I do know you," Sutherland said. He pushed his gun into Zeke's mouth and pulled the trigger. Zeke's blood and brains mixed with those of his boss on the chair and wall.

Sutherland withdrew the gun, walked back through the curtains into the saloon. The place was empty. No one waited around to see what had happened.

Sutherland went behind the bar, took down a bottle of whiskey, and drank straight from it. He was going to have to get rid of Butler before he went after Luke Short. And since the man was out looking for him, maybe the best thing to do was let him find him.

On the other hand, maybe he didn't actually have to kill Butler himself to be in line to collect the price on his head. Maybe it was good enough just to see that Butler was killed.

He took another swig from the bottle, put it back, then took it down again and left, carrying it with him.

When Butler entered the Bloody Spur he knew something was wrong. Nobody was there.

"Zeke?"

He drew his gun and walked across the room to the curtained doorway in the back. He used the barrel of the gun to move the curtains aside, and then entered. He stopped short when he saw the grizzly scene behind the desk.

Butler moved closer. The back of the man's head had been blown out, and then he'd fallen facedown onto the desk. Butler leaned over to get a look at his face without moving him. It was Zeke, killed the way his boss had been killed—by the same man?

Sutherland?

The man had obviously come here straight from the whorehouse. He must have thought it was Zeke who told Butler where to find him.

"Sorry, friend," Butler said.

He had to get out of there fast, just in case the law was on the way. Customers had obviously cleared out when they heard the shot.

Sutherland was trying to wipe out any trail to him, but Butler had the feeling that if he stood still, the man would find him.

# CHAPTER 39

When Butler walked into the White Elephant Saloon he could see from the door the look of relief on Jerry the bartender's face.

As he reached the bar Jerry said, "I was startin' to think you was dead."

"I'll take a beer and we'll drink to me still being alive," Butler said.

"Suits me."

As he was waiting for his beer a hand came down on his shoulder from behind. He turned quickly, thinking it was Sutherland, but it was Luke Short.

"Where the hell have you been?" He asked the question without rancor.

"I had some errands."

"Where?"

"Hell's Half Acre."

"What the hell—"

"Have a beer and I'll fill you in."

Later Short said, "You're crazy, do you know that? You could've got yourself killed."

"Well, somebody got killed, all right," Butler observed.

"Jesus," Short said, "I've got to watch what I say from now on. Threaten to blow one person's head off and suddenly there's an epidemic."

"The sheriff is going to come looking for you again," Butler said. "Get yourself a good alibi."

"I've got one," Short said. "I was here this whole time, right out in front of people."

"We better talk to Al Newman again, just in case," Butler said.

"I can't ask him to help again," Short said.

"You didn't ask him last time," Butler pointed out, "I did."

"Well, nothing's happened yet," Short said. "Let's just wait and see. Meanwhile, what do we do about Sutherland?"

"He's either going to come looking for me," Butler said, "or send somebody."

"Why wouldn't he take you down himself?"

"He had a shot at me tonight," Butler said, "and he didn't take it. There must be a reason. I'm thinking he's going to send some friends to look for me."

"Meanwhile, what's he going to be doing?" Short asked.

"I don't know what's on his mind now," Butler said. "The man who was paying him is dead. Unless he's suddenly got more ambition, Sutherland's pretty much just a gunman for hire."

"Maybe," Short said, "if he starts making his own decisions, he'll make some mistakes.

"Oh, he's made plenty of mistakes, already," Butler

said. "He missed me once, and he killed his boss. Now he's killed Zeke, the bartender. And I was able to find him."

"Do you think you can find him again?" Short asked.

"I wish I knew more about him," Butler said. "If he's got any kind of smarts, he'd set himself up somewhere and wait for me to find him again. Maybe get some help."

"So if he does that, and sets up an ambush, what are you going to do? Walk right into it?"

"I could do that," Butler said, "but then we'd have to have something set up, too."

"Like what?"

"Well, we don't know much about him, but we do know that we're smart," Butler said. "We just have to think about it."

Sutherland had a small room above a dockside saloon that catered only to seamen. He never went down there. He didn't like seamen, but he figured nobody would look for him there.

He entered his room and locked the door behind him. He was still holding the bottle of whiskey in his left hand. He'd kept his right hand free in case he had to go for his gun.

He went to the window and stared down at the docks. He was only a two-block walk from Rosie's, but he wasn't planning on going back there for a while.

He took a deep swallow from the whiskey bottle and turned away from the window. He had to think, and he was the first to admit this wasn't his strong suit. He was a man of action, with somebody else usually doing the thinking, just pointing him in the right direction. But he'd killed Ed Cramer, and there was only one other man in Fort Worth who regularly had use for his talents. He could go to that man and ask for guidance, but he decided to try and think it out himself, first.

He took the bottle of whiskey to bed with him, sucked on it until it was empty, and fell asleep.

# CHAPTER 40

———◆———

Butler woke the next morning to the insistent pressure of a naked hip against his. It was smooth and warm and very pleasurable. He reluctantly rolled away from it then turned over to have a look. Her name was Laura and she'd been sent up to his room by Jerry, who said not to worry about paying her.

Her auburn hair was long and covered her face, which he knew to be lovely. Beneath the covers he knew she had round breasts, rounded hips and buttocks. He told Jerry he did not want a skinny girl.

Sitting between Ruby and Kimmie the night before had been stimulating. And when he got back to the White Elephant he had still been feeling it, so he asked Jerry if he knew of any girls, and Jerry being a bartender, of course he did.

He got out of bed, used the pitcher and basin to wash up, and got dressed. He was strapping on his gun when she rolled over and looked at him.

"You don't want a wake-me-up?" she asked, smiling.

"Nope," he said. "I think I had that a couple of hours ago. I might not survive another one."

He took some money from his pocket, showed it to her, and put it on the dresser.

"Jerry said you weren't supposed to pay."

"Will he pay you?"

"No."

"Is he your pimp?"

"Jerry? No."

"Then you don't have to give any of this to him?" Butler asked.

"Well, no . . ."

"Fine," he said, "then this is just between us."

She sat up and the sheet fell away, exposing her lovely, chubby breasts.

"Are you gonna want me tonight?"

He didn't usually use whores, but last night had been a special case.

"I don't know, Laura," he said, even though he did know. "Can I contact you through Jerry?"

"Sure."

"Then I'll let you know."

"Well . . . okay."

"Thanks," he said.

As he was going out the door she shouted, "Well, take care, then."

Sutherland woke up with a fuzzy tongue and even fuzzier head. He immediately gave up the idea of doing any thinking for himself. He was going to get something to eat and then go see his other employer. He'd lay out the whole situation and listen to what the man had to say. If he didn't want to get involved, fine. Sutherland would just have to try not to get mad and kill the man. He might need him again somewhere down the line. Besides, this really wasn't his problem, anyway. Sutherland had gotten himself into this mess, and he was going to have to get himself out the way he always did.

With a gun.

Butler went downstairs and had breakfast in the White Elephant dining room. The waiter, who knew him by now, automatically brought steak and eggs and coffee.

"Has Mr. Short been in yet?" Butler asked.

"No, sir, not yet."

"Okay, thanks."

"If he comes in would you like me to bring him over?" the young man asked, eager to please the boss's friend.

"Yes, you can do that. Thanks"—he groped for the man's name, and found it—"Philip."

He ate with gusto. Sex was an appetite builder, and sex with Laura had particularly built his appetite. He started to think, why not have her again that night? And then he thought, if I'm alive.

Suddenly, he stopped thinking about Laura and started thinking about Sutherland. Somebody had to know where the man lived. If he was down in Hell's Half Acre all the time he must have a friend, or somebody who at least knew something about him.

Then he thought of Al Newman. Maybe a man who ran for district attorney would know something about the local criminal element.

He decided he would risk the wrath of Mrs. Newman and go see Al after breakfast.

# CHAPTER 41

"Sutherland," the man said, "it sounds like you've gotten yourself into a real mess."

"I guess so."

"I warned you this would happen if you kept working for Ed Cramer."

"Yeah, you did."

"You didn't happen to kill Cramer, did you?" the man asked.

"No," Sutherland lied, "best I know, Luke Short did that."

The man nodded. Sutherland had already told him what Cramer wanted him to do—kill Luke Short—and what he himself had wanted to do—kill Butler for the price on his head, and then kill Short for his reputation.

"And I assume you still want the two things you told me about?" the man asked.

"Yep."

"Short's rep is that important to you?"

"Yeah, and so's the money."

"Which is more important?"

"I need both."

"So if I told you that the best thing for you to do would be to leave town, you wouldn't do it, right?"

"No, I couldn't," Sutherland said.

The man thought a moment, then asked, "Do you have any friends?"

"No."

"Every man has at least one friend."

"Don't need 'em."

"Do you know any men who would help you with this?"

"I know a few."

"Good men?"

"Good at doin' what they're told." Like me, he added to himself, only not as good.

"Okay," the other man said, "give me some time to think it over. How do I get in touch with you?"

"You don't," Sutherland said. "I'll come to you."

"It'll be better if you give me something," the man said. "Doesn't have to be where you live, just some place I could leave a message."

Sutherland thought about the Bloody Spur. But that was out. Finally, he told the man the name of the saloon he lived above, without mentioning that fact.

"You can leave me a message there."

"Okay, good," the man said.

He got up and walked Sutherland to the back door of his home.

"I'm sorry I came to your house," he said, before leaving. "I didn't know any other way."

"It's all right," the man said. "I'll come up with something for you. It'll be all right."

"Thanks."

The man slapped Sutherland on the back and let him out.

Butler knocked on the front door of Al Newman's house. The door was opened by his wife, who gave him a disapproving look.

"Mrs. Newman," he said, quickly, "I'm just here to talk to Al. Honest."

"About what?"

"Helen? Who is it?"

Instead of telling her husband who it was she asked, "Why can't you people leave him alone?" and turned and walked away. In moments Newman appeared.

"Hey, Butler," Newman said. "Come on in. Luke's not in jail again, is he?"

"Not yet," Butler said, entering, "but there was another murder last night."

"Jesus, who?"

"A bartender down at the Bloody Spur. Worked for Ed Cramer. He was killed the same way."

"Come on in. Brandy?"

"Sure," Butler said, even though it was early.

"I know it's early, but this is one of the perks of being retired. I don't have to go to an office today."

He handed Butler a brandy snifter, then sipped from his own.

"What can I do for you today?"

"Just a few questions," Butler said. "You told me you ran for district attorney once."

"Twice," Newman said. "Narrowly defeated both times."

"Well, would this give you any familiarity with the criminal element here in Fort Worth?"

"Yes, it would, plus the fact that I was a criminal attorney here for years."

Butler felt stupid for having forgotten that.

"Why? Are you looking for a criminal?"

"A man named Sutherland," Butler said. "Have you ever heard of him?"

"Local strongarm," Newman said. "Works with a gun, and sometimes his hands."

"You wouldn't happen to know where he lives, would you?"

"Afraid not," Newman said. "I haven't had any personal dealings with the man."

"I see."

"But I would imagine he lives down in Hell's Half Acre somewhere."

"I've looked there. Found a whorehouse he frequents, but not where he lives. Nobody seems to know him that well."

"I guess I could keep my ears open, maybe ask around," Newman said. "One of my old colleagues might know something."

"I'd appreciate it, Al."

"How's Luke doing?" Newman asked as he walked Butler to the front door.

"We're trying to get this worked out so we can all get back to the business of the day."

"Gambling."

"Yes."

Newman laughed as he opened the door.

"Well, keep me in mind."

"Don't worry," Butler said. "I still owe you, so you'll be in the first game we put together."

"Again," Newman said, "sorry about the wife."

"She's got a right to be annoyed," Butler said. "Sounds like you got more people than just me bothering you."

"What?"

"Oh, just something she said."

"What was that?"

"She said, 'Why can't you people leave him be?' or something to that effect. Assumed it meant some other folks had been bothering you with their problems."

"No," Newman said, "just you." He laughed. "I'll have to ask her what she meant by that."

"Well," Butler said, "I didn't mean to start a fight between you two."

"Don't worry about it," Newman said. "Even if we do fight, Helen has a short memory for things like that. She never stays mad long."

"That would make her a rare woman, indeed," Butler said, not believing a word of it.

# CHAPTER 42

As Butler left Al Newman's house he had the feeling that the man had lied to him. Well, not so much a lie, as a bluff. He'd picked up something about Newman at the poker table, and felt that he knew every time the man bluffed—and he was bluffing now.

But about what?

A simple lie about his wife, maybe? He didn't want Butler to think she was a shrew? The woman had displayed no good qualities in Butler's presence, at all. And, apparently, Newman had spoken to her about being rude but she had ignored his counsel.

Or was it something else?

Maybe about Sutherland?

Maybe he knew Sutherland's reputation and wanted to keep Butler from going after him?

Maybe he didn't want Butler dead, because then he'd never get into another of Luke Short's games?

And maybe Butler was just being unfair and Newman was trying to look out for him out of friendship?

When a man bluffed it usually meant he had no hand. In this case, what did it mean?

\* \* \*

"They have to stop coming here, Albert," Helen Newman said to her husband in the kitchen.

"Yes, dear."

"I mean it," she said. "You're not part of that world anymore. And you were never part of that gambling world. I don't like that."

"I know dear."

"I don't like any of them, and I don't want them in my house."

"I'll remember that."

She turned and looked at him.

"You're just yesing me, aren't you, Albert?" she demanded. "You're just going to go on doing what you want to do, aren't you? No Matter what I say?"

He smiled at her and said, "Yes, dear."

She turned her back on him and busied herself at the stove.

"Will you be staying in for lunch today?"

"I believe I will."

She fell silent, then said, "You could at least keep them out of my kitchen."

He came up behind her, took her shoulders, kissed her hair and said, "Yes, dear."

Butler thought he might be reading something into nothing, but he didn't have many other options. Catching Sutherland and proving that he was the killer was the only way to get Luke Short out from under. And it was the only way for him to be able to move on. Things had not gone the way he planned in Fort Worth. Other than that one game—and he had done very well in it—there had been no high-stakes poker. Just like Dodge City and Denver, he'd gotten himself wrapped up in the troubles of his new friends, to the detriment of his poker. He needed to get this matter resolved so he could leave town and head for California before he got himself killed.

He watched as Helen Newman came out of her house, closed the door behind her, and walked away. As far as he knew, Al Newman was still inside. But at the moment he wasn't concerned with Al, he was concerned with Helen.

He left his hiding place, fell in behind her, and started to follow her.

# CHAPTER 43

It was not Butler's intention to follow Mrs. Newman for any period of time. What he wanted to do was find a place where he could approach and speak with her. He certainly had no intention of pulling her into a wall the way he did Walt the night before. He needed something a little more subtle.

He finally just decided to go ahead and approach her while she was shopping. And even though he tried making it look as if they had simply run into each other, she managed to see through that subterfuge very quickly.

"Mr. Butler," she said, "are you following me?"

"No, Mrs. Newman, I just happened—"

"You just happened to be walking by the very millinery shop where I buy my hats?"

He looked up and saw that he had, indeed, "bumped" into her as she was coming out of a hat shop.

"Well," he said, "I guess you caught me, then . . ."

"What is it you wish to talk to me about?"

"Actually, it's about your husband and—"

That was when she cut him off and told him that if he wanted to talk to her, he'd have to accompany her to her next destination.

He never expected it to be a tea room.

"Tea, Mr. Butler?" she asked, after the waitress had left them an entire pot.

"Sure, why not?"

She poured him a cup, and then herself. He dubiously eyed the array of small cakes and sandwiches arranged on a blue china plate, laid out to accompany the tea.

"Watercress sandwich?" she asked.

"Uh, no, thanks," he said. "I had a big breakfast."

"I can never get Albert to come here with me," she said. "He claims it's effeminate. Do you think it's effeminate, Mr. Butler?"

"Ma'am, let's just say I hope no one who knows me passes by and looks in."

"You men," she said. "Always so concerned about what other people think."

"Well, I don't think you can say that just about men, Mrs. Newman," Butler said. "After all, why do you buy all sorts of hats and shoes and dresses and perfumes? Certainly not so you can wear them in your house when you're alone and look in the mirror at yourself."

"Touché, Mr. Butler," she said. "I see there is more to you than meets the eye. You seem so . . . educated."

"I'm not a native westerner, Mrs. Newman."

"Yes, that is becoming apparent," she said. "My husband tells me I've been rude to you on more than one occasion. Let me take this opportunity to . . . apologize, which is not something I do easily."

"Then I appreciate it," he said, "even though I don't think it's necessary."

"Very well," she said. "Since we have that out of the way, and since you won't have something to eat—"

"I will take one of these lemon cakes," he said, after surreptitiously eyeing the entire assortment for something he recognized.

"Ah, good," she said. "The high tea experience is complete, then. Now, tell me Mr. Butler, what is it you wanted to talk to me about?"

"Well . . . it's something you said a while ago, at your front door?"

"I thought I apologized for that already."

"No," he said, "not that. You said, 'I wish you'd all leave him alone.' Who did you mean?"

"Well . . .you, for one. I don't want Albert being brought back into that criminal world."

"Okay, I know you meant me," Butler said, "but who else?"

"Luke Short," she said. "I don't want him in that gambling world, either."

"I get the feeling there was someone else you meant, though."

"Well . . . I don't even know if I should mention it . . . but there was a horrid man who came to call just a little while before you."

"What man? Do you know his name?"

"No, but I know his type," she said.

"What type is that?"

"The criminal type," she said. "The type who lives and works down by the docks."

Butler's heart started to race, the way it did when he thought he knew what cards a man had in his hand.

"Can you describe him?"

"A big, brutish, dirty man—"

"Can you be as little more specific?"

She got more specific and gave him a perfect description of Sutherland. Or rather, a perfect duplicate of the description they had of Sutherland.

So Newman had lied about knowing Sutherland. And not only did he know him, but he had spoken to him—in his home—just before Butler got there.

Very interesting.

# CHAPTER 44

"You're kidding," Luke Short said.

"That's what she said."

"Do you really think it was Sutherland?"

"The description matches perfectly," Butler said. "And as Newman himself pointed out to me, he was a criminal lawyer."

"You know," Short said, "you and me, we don't know much about Newman—but I know who does."

They found Bill Ward in his office and hit him with what Butler had found out. Both Short and Butler expected the man to defend his friend, but instead he just sat there, not looking particularly surprised.

"Bill," Short said, "talk to me."

"What would you have me say?" Ward asked. "That the man was a criminal lawyer, but he didn't associate with criminals? That's ridiculous. Of course he did. What does that prove?"

"It proves he lied to Butler," Short said. "Why would he do that?"

"I honestly don't know," Ward said. "I guess you're just going to have to ask him."

"Maybe we'll do that," Short said, "but Bill, we need you to keep quiet about this and let us handle it."

"I'm only too happy to stay out of it," Ward said. "This is between you and Newman."

After they left the office Butler said, "Do you really think he'll stay out of it?"

"Bill's a man of his word," Short said. "Yeah, I think he will."

"So, do you want to confront Newman with this?" Butler asked.

"I wish I knew what his wife was going to do," Short said. "I wish I knew if she was going to tell him about your conversation with her."

"Well, I didn't act like it was any real revelation," Butler said. "We finished our tea and went our separate ways."

"I really have to thank you, Butler," Short said. "You put yourself on the line for me today."

"Forget it. I—"

"You drank, tea," Short said. "Did she make you lift your pinky up when you took a sip?"

Short laughed long and hard and Butler let him have his enjoyment. He didn't think they'd have very much more to laugh about until they caught Sutherland.

They went to the bar, got a beer each, and continued to discuss the situation.

"Why do you think Sutherland would go to Newman in the first place?" Short asked.

"For help?" Butler suggested. "This is a man not used to doing his own thinking. Maybe he's lost without Cramer. If he didn't realize that would be the case when he killed Cramer, he realizes it now. So he goes to Newman to see if he can help him figure out what to do."

"Why wouldn't Newman turn him over to the law?" Short asked. "After all, this is a man who ran for district attorney. He knows the law."

"Maybe he's got the same opinion of Courtwright that you do."

"Could be," Short said. "So what's he going to tell Sutherland to do?"

"I don't know," Butler said.

"And how do we find Sutherland?"

"By watching Newman," Butler said. "He's bound to go back to him."

"Unless Newman's wife tells him about you."

Butler rubbed his jaw.

"This is delicate. If we go to Newman and confront him he may warn Sutherland, and we'll never catch him. What if he decides to leave town?"

"Then I'm dead," Short said. "I'm the one they'll pin both killings on."

"Let's remember he took a shot at me," Butler said. "That can only be because of the price I carry and I don't think he'd want to give that up."

"Probably not," Short said. "Or maybe he was just trying to get you out of the way so he'd have a clear run at me."

"Either way," Butler said, "whether he wants the money or your rep, he's not leaving town without it. Not when he's gone this far."

"I hope you're right."

Butler hoped so, too.

# CHAPTER 45

———◆◆◆———

Sutherland had to pick a new place to meet with the men he'd chosen. Normally, it would have been the Bloody Spur, but with both its owner and bartender having been killed, the place was now boarded up.

He chose a saloon called the Black Pearl, and had three men meet him there. He bought them all beers and they sat at a back table.

"What's on your mind, Sutherland?" Lenny Randolph asked.

Randolph and Harry Spills were partners, did everything together. They were notoriously cheap, and had even been known to share the same whore. They were both in their mid-thirties.

The third man he'd chosen was Andy Dennis, a loner in his early thirties who was known to do anything for money—the right amount of money.

Sutherland didn't know how much money he had to pass around. He had plans to break into the Bloody Spur, where he knew Ed Cramer kept cash in the office. He only hoped that Zeke hadn't already found it.

Of course, he could share the bounty on Butler with

his "friends." There was plenty to go around, providing he gave them each just a taste.

He could string them along for the money for a while. But first he had to find out if they were willing to work with him—or for him.

"You don't usually need help with your jobs," Andy Dennis said. "What gives?"

"I've got two things going, so I may need help with one of them."

"What're these deals?" Randolph asked.

"Does this have anything to do with Ed Cramer, over at the Bloody Spur?" Spills asked.

Everyone went silent.

"What about Cramer?" Sutherland asked.

"Uh, well, you used to work for him, is all," Spills said. "I was just wondering if this was a job for him that you're finishin' up?"

Sutherland sat quietly and stared at Spills.

"I didn't mean nothin' by it," Spills finally said. "I was just askin'."

"This has nothin' to do with Cramer," Sutherland said. "This is all me."

"Okay," Spills said.

"Let me explain . . ."


"I don't think we have a choice," Butler said.

"We have to confront Al Newman. If he's an honest man, he'll help us catch Sutherland."

"And if he's not?" Short asked.

"Then he'll try and set us up for Sutherland."

"And how will we know which way he's going?" Short asked.

"We'll have to use our instincts, Luke," Butler said. "Our poker-playing instincts."

"You think we can succeed if we apply those away from the table?"

"It's already worked for me a couple of times," Butler said, "maybe more. Anyway, I really don't have the time or patience to wait, do you?"

"Hell, no," Short said. "I want to get on with my life."

"So do I," Butler replied, "so let's go and talk to him."

# CHAPTER 46

"Let me get this straight," Andy Dennis said. "You want us to take care of this Butler while you kill Luke Short?"

"That's right."

"And when we do it you'll pay us?" Spills asked. "Out of the reward?"

He'd told them several times there was no reward, but they couldn't get it through their heads. *Reward* was the only word they understood.

"Right."

"And the reward is how much, again?" Randolph asked.

"I didn't say," Sutherland replied. "I just told you what I was gonna pay each of you. That's all you need to know."

"So you get to keep most of the reward," Spills said, "and you get a reputation when you kill Luke Short."

"What's the difference?" Dennis asked. "Short's probably gonna kill 'im."

"That's a possibility," Sutherland said.

"Then," Dennis said, "we should probably get some-thin' up front. You know, to make it worth our time."

"Okay," Sutherland said, "I'll get you—give you some money."

"Each?" Spills asked.

"Each."

"How much?" Randolph asked.

"Meet me here tomorrow, same time," Sutherland said, "and I'll have the cash."

The men exchanged a glance, then Dennis said, "Well, okay."

Satisfied that their business was concluded, the three of them got up and left. Sutherland noticed as they went through the batwing doors that Andy Dennis went to the left, while Spills and Randolph went to the right.

He sat back in his chair, eyeing his unfinished beer. He was going to have to break into Cramer's office at the Bloody Spur tonight and hopefully find some money to pay those three. With any luck nothing would have to come out of his own pocket.

He downed his beer, got up and left, heading for the boarded up Bloody Spur.

Butler and Short had one more drink that night before deciding to turn in. Butler was heading for the comfort of his bed, Short had to go upstairs to the casino and close it out.

Having second thoughts, Butler asked, "You want me to come up with you?"

"No," Short said, "I tend to think I'm pretty safe in here."

"You're letting men with guns come in, you know," Butler reminded him.

"A man with a gun right in front of me, in my face, I can handle," Short said. "So what's the plan for tomorrow?"

"I think we should catch Newman outside his home, surprise him the way I did Mrs. Newman, and hit him with what we know. Then we can take it from there."

"Okay," Short said. "So let's meet up at eight A.M., get a little breakfast, and then go and find him."

"He's retired—technically—so he probably doesn't leave his home very early. We should be able to catch him."

"What if he doesn't leave his house all day?" Short asked.

"Then we'll change the plan and go in," Butler said. "We'll have to be flexible."

"I can do that," Short said. "I can be flexible."

"Good," Butler said. "I'll see you in the morning, then."

Butler went to his room. Short went to the casino.

Sutherland forced the back door of the Bloody Spur, found his way into Cramer's office. He ignored the stain of Cramer's blood mixed with Zeke's on the chair and wall and began to search. It didn't take long before he found a metal box in the bottom drawer of Cramer's desk. It was locked, so he pried it open pretty easily and found it was filled with cash. He counted; there was enough to pay the three men without having to touch any of his own money.

He pocketed the cash, was about to leave, then decided to go out into the saloon. He went around behind the bar, grabbed a bottle of whiskey, opened it, and took a long pull. He remembered that he had given out the name of the saloon he lived above as a place to leave messages. He didn't go in there often, but he knew the owner and one of the bartenders because they'd run into each other from time to time, coming and going. He was going to have to stop in there and remind them that they had agreed to pass on any news meant for him. Actually, it would probably only be one message. He took another swig from the bottle, corked it, put it back, then grabbed it and took it with him when he left.

# CHAPTER 47

━━━◆◆◆━━━

After breakfast Butler and Short took a cab to Al Newman's neighborhood. They found a doorway down the street from his home and waited.

After an hour Short said, "This is starting to feel silly."

"How so?"

"I'm loitering in a doorway with you," Short said. "Somebody might notice the two of us here and send for the law."

Butler studied the establishment whose doorway they were standing in. It was a leather shop, and according to a sign in the window it would be opening in half an hour.

"We're going to have to move, anyway," Butler said, but before he could say why, Short cut him off. "Look."

The front door of Newman's house opened and he came walking out. He was wearing a light jacket and a hat; he headed down the street away from them.

"Let's split up and follow him," Butler said. "I'll do it from across the street."

"Okay," Short said, "but if he spots me we'll have to make one of those quick decisions you were talking about."

"Fine."

They followed him for two hours without either of them being spotted. He stopped in a cigar store, a telegraph office, a saloon for one beer, and a restaurant for something to eat.

Butler crossed over and stood next to Short as they looked in the window of the small café.

"Maybe we should have braced him in the telegraph office," Short said. "Maybe he was in there because of something to do with us."

"I say we go in now, while he's eating," Butler said, "catch him off guard."

"And have some coffee," Short added. "I could use some coffee."

"So could I."

"You do the talking," Short said. "He feels friendlier toward you, since you're the one who got him into the game."

"Okay," Butler said, "just follow my lead."

He opened the door and they walked in, approached Newman's table. The man was enjoying a cup of coffee and slice of pie. He looked up. Butler thought he looked momentarily annoyed, but then he plastered a smile across his face.

"Butler, Luke," he said. "What are you two doing here?"

"Somebody told me this was a good place for pie," Butler said. "And then this morning Luke said he was in the mood for pie. So . . ." Butler spread his hands.

He did not see the pained look on Short's face, but his explanation sounded lame even to him.

"Well, whoever told you that was right," Newman said. "Sit down and join me. I'm having apple, but the peach is just as good."

When the middle-aged waitress came over, Butler ordered peach and coffee while Short asked for coffee and apple.

"How are you guys doing trying to scare up a game?" Newman asked.

"Not well," Butler said. "We still have this problem of trying to find Sutherland."

"Suther—oh, that man you told me about yesterday," Newman said.

"That's right," Butler agreed. "You said you'd keep your ears open, check with some of your contacts."

"I'm sorry, fellas," Newman said, "I've come up with nothing on the man."

Butler made his decision quickly. He didn't want the pause to stretch out too long.

"That's funny, Al."

"Why do you say that?"

"We have information that says you know Sutherland," Butler said.

"Is that a fact?"

"Furthermore, that he was in your house just before I arrived, yesterday."

Newman put his fork down and sat back. Both men were looking at him. The waitress came with their pie and they waited for her to dole it out before they spoke again.

"Who told you this?" Newman asked.

It seemed apparent now that Newman's wife had not gone home and told him about her conversation with Butler.

"Just a source," Butler said. "You know about sources, right?"

"Oh, yes. I know about sources. I know that some are reliable and some aren't."

"Oh, well, this one's pretty reliable," Butler said.

"So what would you say if I told you your source was wrong?" Newman asked. "That I don't know Sutherland and that he certainly has never been in my house?"

"Well, Al," Butler said, "I guess I'd say you were bluffing, and I'd have to call you on it."

# CHAPTER 48

———◆———

"You don't know me well enough to call me a liar, Butler," Al Newman said.

"I beg to differ. I've spent hours with you at a poker table. I'm fully qualified to call you a liar."

Newman looked at Short.

"And you?"

"I haven't played poker with you at all," Short said, "but I'll go along with Butler on this."

"So," Newman asked, "what happens if I try to walk out of here?"

"We'll stop you," Butler said. "We need some answers from you, and you're not going anywhere until we get them."

"One way or another," Short added.

Newman eyed them each for a moment, then said, "You two make a good team."

"That's flattering to hear," Butler said, "but it doesn't help our situation."

Newman took a deep breath but with a pleasant look on his face. He'd gotten very lucky at the tables that night. The cards had been running his way, but Butler hoped he'd been a better lawyer than he was a poker player. He couldn't bluff worth a damn.

"All right," he said, "I do know Sutherland from my days as a criminal lawyer, but not well."

"And he came to you?" Butler asked. "Why?"

"Out of desperation, I guess. Apparently Ed Cramer used to tell him what to do, and without that—guidance—he seems lost."

"So he wants you to tell him what to do?" Butler asked.

"Apparently so."

"And what did you tell him?" Short asked.

"I said I'd think it over and get in touch with him later."

"And have you thought it over?"

"Yes."

"And?"

"I was going to talk to Jim Courtwright today."

"So you know where Sutherland is, then?" Butler asked.

"No," Newman said, "but he gave me a place to send messages to."

"Where?" Butler asked.

"A saloon down near the docks."

"Al, did he say that he'd killed Cramer?" Short asked the lawyer.

"No," Newman said. "On the contrary, he said he didn't, but he thought you had."

Short looked at Butler.

"That's got to be a lie. I know I didn't kill Cramer, so who else could it be?"

"There are lots of murderers down there," Newman

said. "Men who will cut down any man for a few dollars. Cramer must've got on the wrong side of at least one of them."

"Maybe . . ." Short said.

"Okay, Al," Butler said. "So why lie to me about knowing Sutherland?"

Newman raised his hands helplessly.

"You hit me with that about a half hour after he left my house," Newman said. "You caught me unaware. I wasn't sure what I was going to do. So I lied. I'm sorry."

Butler studied Newman, who he felt was contriving to look embarrassed.

"Okay, so you're supposed to leave him a message at this saloon, and then what?"

"I guess that would depend on what the message was," Newman said. "I could tell him not to bother me anymore."

"Or you could tell him to meet you somewhere," Short said, "and we could be there."

"I thought I might do that and the law would be there to grab him."

"If Courtwright thought he could kill Sutherland and still be able to pin the murders on me, he would," Short said. "We need to be able to catch him and turn him in ourselves."

"And have somebody from the *Evening Mail* or some other newspaper present," Butler suggested.

"Well," Newman said, "where would you like me to have him meet you?"

"You'll do it?" Butler asked.

"Why not? If he actually killed the two men your being blamed for, Luke, I'd like to help."

Butler still wasn't sure about Newman. This could have been his way of getting rid of Sutherland so the man could not implicate him in anything further.

"Luke?" Butler asked. "You know this town better than I do."

"Why not the Bloody Spur?" Short asked. "It's boarded up, now."

Would that be someplace Al Newman would go, Butler wondered?

"Let's try and think of someplace else," Butler suggested. "Someplace Sutherland would think Al would go."

"It would have to be someplace we'd both go," Newman said, "so that neither one of us stood out."

"What about your home again?" Butler asked.

"No," Newman said, "I already told him I did not want him coming back, he upset Helen."

"As I did," Butler said.

"That's quite different," Newman said. "He frightened her."

"Okay," Butler said, "we can decide on the time and place. What should this message say?"

They all sat silent for a while, and then Newman said, "How about. . . I've figured out what he can do and will explain it to him when he meets me."

"Good," Butler said, looking at Luke.

"That's what he wants to hear," Short replied.

"Let's do it now," Newman suggested.

"Here?" Short asked.

"Why not? I'll have the waitress bring me a pencil and paper."

"And who will deliver the message?" Newman asked.

"Can't be one of us," Short said. "We'll be recognized."

"We'll find somebody," Newman said. "A kid will do it for four bits."

"We appreciate your willingness to cooperate, Al," Short said.

"Think nothing of it," he said, waving to the waitress to get her attention.

# CHAPTER 49

Spills, Randolph, and Dennis had no other place to pick up Butler except at the White Elephant. They did not, however, get there in time to see him leave in the morning with Luke Short. So they were all surprised when they saw Butler and Luke Short come walking back in later in the day. Short was easy to recognize because of his hat and cane—and, in fact, Dennis had seen him before. Butler they recognized because he was with Short, and from the description Sutherland had given them.

"Okay, so now he's back inside," Randolph said to the other two. "What do we do now?"

"We could go in," Spills said, "start an argument, gun 'im and get out."

"Too much chance someone else will get involved," Dennis said to them. "We gotta get 'im outside, when he's alone."

"He might be right," Randolph said. "He's gotta have friends in there."

They were across the street and Dennis said, "We've

got to wait in front of the place. We don't wanna have to run across the street when he comes out."

"Okay," Randolph said, "let's get over there. Me and Spills can stand on one side of the door, and you on the other.

Dennis had heard the stories about these guys doing everything together.

"That's fine," Dennis said. "Just don't start firing until I do."

He thought he might get an argument from the two of them, but they seemed perfectly satisfied with being told what to do.

As they crossed the street, though, Randolph did have one question.

"Whatta we do if he doesn't come out tonight?"

"We'll just have to deal with that if it happens," Dennis said. "Right now let's stick to this plan."

"Okay," Randolph said, "whatever ya say."


"This is the damn part I hate again," Short said, when he and Butler got inside.

"What part's that?" Butler asked.

"The waiting."

They were at the bar, each with a beer in front of them, but neither of them was really interested.

"I know what you mean, Luke," Butler said. "It's especially hard when you're waiting to hear from somebody you don't trust."

"You didn't buy what he was selling, either?"

"Not for a minute," Butler said. "The man is a terrible liar, just like he's a terrible bluffer at the table."

"So why are we waiting?"

"Either way," Butler said, "something's going to happen. Either he'll set Sutherland up, or he'll try to set us up, or Sutherland will just come here for us."

"I think I'd prefer the last," Short said. "I like being on home ground."

"Well, this is certainly your home, and downtown is Sutherland's home ground."

"So where's your home ground?"

"I'm afraid I don't have one," Butler said. "For the time being, maybe I can just borrow yours."

# CHAPTER 50

Jerry had not told his bosses or Butler, but he had decided to take the initiative. He had put a man across the street from the White Elephant, just to keep an eye on things. He'd told Tim Doocey to let him know if he saw anything suspicious. Doocey wasn't really clear on what Jerry would consider to be suspicious, but he had a feeling three men with guns loitering around the front doors qualified. Especially since they had started out across the street.

Doocey walked down the block, crossed the street, went down an alley, and entered the White Elephant through a back door. He made his way across the busy floor to the bar, got Jerry's attention and told him what he saw. Jerry slapped the young man on the back and gave him a free beer. Then he went around the bar to where Butler and Luke Short were still standing.

"There's three men with guns outside the front door," Jerry said. "They look like they're waitin' for somethin'—or someone."

"How do you know?" Short asked.

Jerry told them about putting Tim Doocey across the street, just in case.

"Jerry," Short said, "I think you deserve a raise . . ."

"Thanks, Boss."

". . . and probably a promotion. I'm going to talk to Bill Ward about it."

"Thanks. Do you, uh, want me to get my shotgun?" the bartender asked.

"No," Short said. "Just stay where you are and do your job. Where's Doocey?"

"End of the bar," Jerry said. "I gave him a free beer. He's happy."

"How old is he?"

"About twenty-two, I think."

"We'll put him on the payroll," Short said, "but don't tell him yet."

"Sure, boss."

"Jerry," Butler asked, "go ask Doocey where the men are exactly."

"Right." Jerry ran down the bar, asked the question, got the answer and came back.

"He says two to the right, one to the left."

"Okay, thanks."

Jerry went down the bar to serve drinks and Short looked at Butler.

"You know what I'm thinkin'?" he asked.

"Yeah," Butler said, "that they're here for me."

"I'm going out the back," Short said. "Give me five minutes and then come out the front."

"Okay."

"You want the two or the one?" Short asked.

That was a tough question. If he said the one it meant

he didn't think he could handle two. And he sure as hell didn't want to admit that to Luke Short.

"If they're here for me, I should take two," he said, finally, "but why don't we try to take your one alive? Maybe we can find out for sure why they're here, and who sent them?"

"Okay," Short said, "as long as you're sure you can take the two."

"Just take care of your guy, Luke," Butler said, "and try not to kill him."

"You know, I really think that's going to be up to him."

Luke Short left the bar and made his way across the saloon floor, pretty much retracing Tim Doocey's steps.

Butler stepped to the front of the saloon and peered out a window. He saw two men waiting together, didn't see the third. That was okay, he had to trust the third to Luke Short. His job was these two.

He took his gun out, checked it, and slid it back into the holster, testing it to see if it would come out easily. Butler knew his real skill was with cards, but he knew he could handle himself with a gun. If these two men were out to ambush him, they were going to be pretty shocked when he came out the batwing doors facing them.

The outcome was going to rely solely on how they reacted.

He waited the full five minutes before walking to the front doors.

Trusting that Luke Short would be where he said he was going to be, Butler walked through the batwing doors. He turned quickly to face the two men who—as he hoped and half expected—seemed completely shocked.

"I think you boys are out here waiting for me," he said.

# CHAPTER 51

"What the fuck—" Randolph said.

"Jesus!" Spills shouted, startled.

Both of them tried to look past Butler at Andy Dennis, but he was nowhere to be found.

"Crap," Randolph said.

He probably would have lived had his partner Spills not panicked and gone for his gun. Butler had no time to differentiate between who was going to shoot and who wasn't. He drew his own gun, shot Spills first. Randolph was saying, "No, no, no wait," even as he tried to draw his own gun. Butler wasted no time shooting him in the chest, knocking him off the boardwalk and into the street.

He turned quickly to see where the third man was. At that moment Luke Short stepped from the alley with a man at the point of his gun.

"This one gave up his gun pretty easily," Short announced. The gun in question had been tucked into Short's belt.

"You sneaked up on me like an injun," the man complained. "Gimme my gun and face me and we'll see who's still standin'."

"Sorry, friend," Short said. "I sneaked up on you to save your life. We need to ask you some questions."

"I ain't answerin' no questions," Dennis said. "I don't know what's goin' on. Me and my friends was just standin' out here mindin' our own business when you and him," he pointed to Butler, "come out blastin'. You killed my friends. Where's the law?"

"We're the only law you have to worry about," Butler said.

"You can't do that."

"Yeah, we can," Short said. He looked past the man at Butler. "Should we take him inside?"

"I don't know," Butler said, scratching his chin with his gunsight. "If we take him inside we can't ever let him out again. We'll have to question him, and then kill him."

"What the hell—" Andy Dennis said. "Whataya talkin' about? Why do you got to kill me?"

"Well," Butler said, "maybe we don't have to."

"Maybe," Short said, from behind the man, "we just want to."

"Jesus—" Dennis said.

"You got two choices," Butler said. "Answer questions out here and live—"

"—or go inside and die," Short said.

Andy Dennis took a deep breath, then asked, "Whataya wanna know?"

By the time they got their questions answered, Sheriff Jim Courtwright had arrived on the scene.

"Now you've done it, Short," he announced. "Shootin' men down in the street."

"Sorry to disappoint you, Sheriff," Butler said, "but Luke never fired a shot."

"Huh?"

"I killed these jaspers," Butler said. "They tried to rob me as I came out of the saloon."

"The hell you say?" Courtwright shot back. "You coverin' for Short, Butler?"

"Just ask this fella," Butler said, pointing to Andy Dennis, whose gun—albeit unloaded—was back in his holster. "He was just passing by and saw the whole thing."

Courtwright glared at Dennis.

"What've you got to say?"

"It's like he said, Sheriff," Andy Dennis said, "they tried to rob him and he got the best of them."

"And what're you doin' out here, Short?" Courtwright demanded.

"I heard the shootin' and came out to see if I could help, Sheriff. That's all."

Courtwright studied the three men intensely, then looked at the two men on the ground. They could see he was torn. He turned to the two deputies standing behind him.

"Get rid of these bodies."

"Yes, sir."

Courtwright looked at Short.

"The bartender at Cramer's place was killed just the way he was."

"I've got an alibi," Short said. "I was here with a saloon full of people."

"How do you know when it happened?"

"It's all over the street, Sheriff," Short said. "Everyone knows."

Courtwright said, "I ain't done with you, yet." Then turned to Butler. "You, neither." He looked at Dennis, said nothing, then turned and stormed away.

"Can I go now?" Dennis asked. "I backed up your story, and told you what you wanted to know."

"Yes, you did," Short said. "You can go as long as you know if we ever see you again, we'll kill you. Got it?"

"I got it," Dennis said, and slunk away.

"He's going to have to get out of town before Sutherland can kill him, too," Butler said.

"Sutherland won't have a chance," Short said, "because we're going to take care of him first."

———◆———

# CHAPTER 52

Luke Short and Butler went to Al Newman's house and, right on the doorstep, Butler said, "Send your message to Sutherland. Tell him to meet you at that saloon on the docks. It's as good a place as any."

"All right," Newman said. "When?"

"Tomorrow," Short said. "Make it noon. It'll give us time to get down there and set up."

"Set up?"

"We're going to try to take him alive," Short said, "so he can clear me."

"All right," Newman said. "I'll get it sent over right away."

"Good," Short said. "Thanks."

"Uh, has something happened since we met last?" Newman asked.

"No," Short said, "nothing special."

They had found out what they wanted to know from Andy Dennis—that it was Sutherland who sent the three of them to kill Butler.

"He wanted us to take care of you," he said to Butler,

then looked at Short and said, "and he's gonna kill you himself."

"He is, huh?" Short asked. "Well, he'll get his chance soon enough."

So now they had Sutherland set up to meet them at this saloon on the docks—or did they?

"You still don't trust Al much, do you?" Butler asked Short.

"No, do you?"

"No," Butler said. "The message we want him to send and the message he does send may be very different."

"We'll have to be ready for anything, then."

"Maybe," Short said, "we should go down there tonight and have a look."

"Okay," Butler said, "but you have to do something about the way you're dressed."

Short looked down at himself, touched his silk hat and said, "There's nothin' wrong with the way I'm dressed."

"I know," Butler said, "that's the problem."

Once again Butler had left his gambler's suit behind in favor of his trail clothes. He looked just fine, he thought, but Luke Short looked woefully out of place and uncomfortable in his plain trousers and cotton shirt.

The saloon Al Newman had told them about turned out to be a sailor's pub called The Anchor. They entered and stopped just inside the door. They must have looked normal enough, because although they garnered a few glances, nobody seemed to have their nose out of joint.

"Jesus," Short said, "don't drink anything."

"I know."

They decided to order two whiskeys, take them to a table, sit for a short time, and then leave. They really just wanted to scope the place out ahead of time.

The bartender was a beefy man in his fifties with hairy forearms and a salt-and-pepper beard. His head was bald and he wore an earring in one ear.

"What'll ya have, mates?"

"Whiskey," Butler said, "for both of us."

The man put two shot glasses on the bar and filled them. Butler paid, and they took their drinks to a back table, as planned.

The place was only half full, at a time when the White Elephant was overflowing with patrons.

"Not much going on here," Short said.

There was no gambling, and not a Stetson in sight. The clientele was all seamen.

"Neither one of us knows what Sutherland looks like," Butler said. "All we have are some descriptions."

"And nobody here fits those."

"Not much more to accomplish here," Butler said. "Let's go."

As they stood up to leave, three men who had been sitting at a table together stood up and barred their exit.

"Whatsa matter, ya don't like our whiskey?" one of them asked.

"The whiskey's fine," Butler said.

"How do ya know? Ya didn't even drink it."

"Ya can't leave without drinkin' it," the second man said.

"That's jes' rude," the third man said.

The three of them seemed able-bodied and not too drunk. In a fight Butler wasn't sure he and Short could handle them, and they certainly didn't want to have to shoot them. And most of all they didn't want to attract undue attention.

"Okay," Butler said, "we'll drink the whiskey."

He went back to the table, lifted the glass and drank while Short watched him as if he was crazy.

The whiskey was cheap and burned all the way down.

"Now your friend," one of the seamen said.

"Ya come to our bar, ya drink our whiskey," one of the others said.

Short walked to the table.

"Drink it and let's get out of here," Butler said under his breath.

Short gave him a murderous look, lifted the glass and drained it.

"There ya go," one of the men said, slapping Short on the back. "That weren't so bad, were it?"

"No," Short said, "it wasn't so bad."

The three men stepped aside and actually ushered Butler and Short through the door. From outside they could hear the men laughing.

"I should go back in and—" Short started, but Butler cut him off.

"We did what we came to do," he said. "We had a look. Let's just go."

"I can't get this taste out of my mouth," Short said, sticking out his tongue. "Yeah, let's get back to the White Elephant so I can have a real drink."

*   *   *

Sutherland entered the Anchor late that night and went directly to the bartender. It was his second time there in so many days.

"Anything come in for me?" he asked.

"Yeah," the bald barman said. "Got it right here." He reached under the bar and pulled out an envelope that now was covered with wet circles.

"Thanks. Lemme have a beer."

Sutherland took the envelope to a table with his beer. He read the message from the lawyer, Al Newman. He'd already heard what had happened in front of the White Elephant Saloon, and knew that Butler wasn't dead. So they were going to come for him tomorrow.

Good. He'd be ready.

He stood up and started to leave, but three men barred his exit.

"You didn't finish yer beer," one said.

"That's rude," a second said.

Before the third man could speak, Sutherland hit him square in the jaw with his fist. The other two men were stunned at the speed with which their friend hit the floor, but before they could act, Sutherland hit one, and grabbed the other, tossing him across the room.

"Anybody else want me to drink my beer?" he asked.

Nobody responded. He started to leave, then something occurred to him. He turned to face the room again.

"Who wants to make some money?"

# CHAPTER 53

Butler and Luke Short had a long breakfast away from the White Elephant. They didn't want any more surprises waiting outside the front door.

"Let's have the cab drop us off a few blocks away and walk the rest," Butler suggested.

"I'm with you," Short said. "Check out the area on the way."

"Right."

Short sat back in his chair, took his cup with him, and regarded Butler across the rim.

"There's a couple of big gamblers comin' in next week," he said. "Johnny Speck, Ed Bradley, and Dick Clark will still be in town. I can get up a big game."

"Al Newman?"

"No," Short said. "No matter how this comes out, not Al Newman."

"Well," Butler said, "however this turns out, I think I'll be back on the trail next week."

"I guess I can understand that," Short said. "I guess this hasn't been the stopover you thought it would be. I'm sorry."

"Not your fault."

"Oh, I wasn't taking the blame," Short said. "I'm just sorry it all happened."

"So am I."

"But at least I can tell Bat and Wyatt when I see them," Short went on, "that we have a good friend in common."

"Yep," Butler replied, "you can certainly say that."

They approached the Anchor at eleven fifty-five. They hadn't seen any sign that they were being watched or followed once the cab had dropped them off.

"This area looks dead now," Butler said.

"Sailors are back on their ships, dockworkers are at work," Short said.

They approached the front door.

"What if they're not open?" Butler asked.

"We'll pound on the door," Short said.

But the place was open, and they went right inside. As they crossed the threshold, the door slammed shut behind them.

The bartender was behind the bar, bald head gleaming. Around the room about half a dozen men stood, armed with boat hooks, clubs, and a couple of guns. The bartender was bouncing a huge club in and out of the palm of his hand.

"Well," Short said, looking around, "I guess we know where Al Newman stands."

# CHAPTER 54

"Welcome back, gents," the bartender said. "We arranged a little reception for you."

"You didn't have to do that," Butler assured them.

"Oh, but we wanted to."

"No," Short said, "I don't think you wanted to. I think you were paid to."

"What's the difference?" the bartender asked. "You're here, we're here. Let's have some fun."

"I don't think that a bar fight where we're outnumbered more than three-to-one is much fun," Butler said. "I think we'll pass."

He tried the door behind him, found it locked.

The bartender smiled widely, revealing large, well-cared for teeth.

"We insist you stay."

The circle of men behind them started to close in. Butler drew his gun and fired. The top half of a club in one man's hand flew off. That stopped their progress.

"Here's how it's going to work," Luke Short said. "You're all going to put your weapons down, and then we'll talk."

The man with half a club in his hand was staring at it. The two men present wearing guns put their hands on their weapons.

"You were probably told to hurt us, maybe kill us," Butler said, "and make it look like a bar fight. If you two men touch your guns, we'll kill you."

Their hands froze near their weapons.

"I've got them," Butler said, so Short looked at the bartender, who was still holding his club.

"Sutherland put you up to this, didn't he?" he asked.

The big man blinked, looked around the room and said, "I still think we can take you."

"I don't think you'll be alive to find out," Short said. "We could all put our weapons down and have an old-fashioned bar fight, but you know what? We don't want to. We don't have the time."

The bartender glared at him.

"If you had any balls you would."

"Well, that's just stupid," Short said. "Let's see who's got balls. You and your friends come ahead, and I'll kill you first. You'll never see if we fall or not."

"You move your hand any closer to that gun, friend, and you're dead," Butler said to one of the armed men. "In fact, drop your guns, both of you."

The two men looked to the bartender for guidance.

"Your call," Short said to him.

The bartender looked angry.

"He said you wouldn't shoot unarmed men."

"He knew we would," Butler said, "to save our lives. He set us all up so some of us would die. You get paid enough for that?"

Now the two men exchanged anxious looks.

"Ah," Short said to Butler, "they haven't been paid yet."

"He knew some of you wouldn't be alive to get paid when this was all done," Butler explained. "How do you all feel about that?"

"What do you say, friend?" Short asked the bartender. "We going to do this or not?"

When there was no answer, Butler said, "Okay, no more playing around. Guns on the floor—now!"

The two hesitated only a moment, then drew their guns from their belts and dropped them to the floor.

"Now, the rest of you drop whatever weapons you're holding."

Hooks, clubs, and knives hit the floor.

"You, too, baldy," Short said to the bartender.

The man continued to glare at Short, then tossed his club over the bar. As it hit the floor he came out with a shotgun from beneath the bar. Apparently, he figured Short would watch the club in its flight and he'd be able to take both him and Butler with one shotgun blast.

His plan didn't work. Short had spent too many years watching the man doing the bluffing, and not the cards on the table.

He drew and fired. The bullet hit the bald man in the chest. He coughed, dropped his shotgun, and then fell to the floor behind the bar.

"Anybody else?" Butler asked.

The other six men all shook their heads.

"Now, we think we know who hired you for this,"

Short said, "but somebody better step up and give us a name, or a description."

One of the men did just that—stepped forward and said, "You got it right, Mister. His name's Sutherland."

"You happen to know where he is now?" Butler asked.

"No, sir," the man said, "but I can tell you where he lives."

He pointed his index finger at the ceiling.

# CHAPTER 55

Butler kicked in the door and Short went in with his gun out.

"Not here," he said.

"How can you tell?"

"It's one damn room."

Butler stuck his head in the door and saw for himself. He had his gun in hand, as he was covering from the back.

"Then where is he?" he asked.

"I don't know," Short said, "but we're going to find him."

They looked at each other.

"Newman?" Butler asked.

"Newman," Short said, with a nod.

They went back down the stairs and away from the docks, where they could find a cab.

Sutherland watched as Butler and Luke Short entered the Anchor, and a couple of dockworkers came running out, slammed the doors behind them, and locked them from the outside. Then he waited and when he heard the first shot knew that things had gone wrong.

Later, when he heard the second shot, he assumed the bartender had gone for the shotgun he kept beneath the bar. The bald, earring-wearing man had told Sutherland, "Worse comes to worse I'll just use my greener shotgun on both of 'em."

Yeah, right . . .

After the second shot he watched as Butler and Luke Short came out and went up the stairs to his room. Butler kicked in the door and Short went in while Butler kept watch outside.

While they were standing in his doorway talking, probably discussing their next move, Sutherland was pretty sure he knew what it would be. He left his hiding place and hurried away, determined to get there ahead of them.

This whole business was going to come to an end today, one way or another.

# CHAPTER 56

As Butler and Luke Short approached the Newman home, they noticed a curtain in one of the front windows move. Someone was watching them.

"Okay," Short said, "so where would we expect to find Sutherland right now?"

"Here?" Butler asked.

"Why not? We came running straight here from the Anchor. What if he was outside, watching?"

"Then he knew that things didn't go the way he planned," Butler said.

"We go knocking on that door now he could start shooting right through it."

"You honestly think Newman would go along with that?" Butler asked.

"Honestly?" Short asked. "That's an odd word to use in this situation. Newman's been anything but honest with us. You know he had to have tipped Sutherland off that we'd be in that saloon, otherwise why would there have been a reception party for us?"

They stood together, staring at the house a few moments.

"I guess one of us could go around the back," Butler said, "and we could go in both ways at the same time."

"And if he's not in there, we'll scare Newman's wife half to death."

"What other options do we have?" Butler asked.

Short stared at the house and tried to think of an answer.

Sutherland watched the two men through the front window, saw them stop short of approaching the house. He'd been hoping they'd just come right up to the door and knock. He turned and looked at Al Newman and his wife, sitting on the sofa in their living room.

"Shouldn't be too much longer, folks," he told them.

While Sutherland continued to watch out the front window, Helen Newman leaned over and hissed at her husband angrily.

"How could you get us mixed up in something like this?"

"Helen," he said, "it was dealing with men like Sutherland that bought us this house."

"I don't care, Albert," she said. "Does that mean we have to let him in our home? Be threatened to our faces? At gunpoint."

"The sheriff should be here soon."

"A lot of good he's going to do us if we're dead," she said. "What does this man want?"

"He wants Luke Short," Newman said, "but he's got to get rid of Butler to get to him."

"Luke Short? Butler? Why do we care about any of them?"

"Because they're professional gamblers."

She waited, and when he didn't say anything else she said, "And?"

How could he explain to her how humiliating it was to stand in that White Horse Saloon week after week and watch lesser men be invited into Luke Short's games. A woman wouldn't understand. Especially a woman like Helen Newman would never understand.

Before he could try and explain his thinking to her, Sutherland said from the window, "Here comes the law." He turned and looked at Al Newman. "Now let's see if your plan works."

Helen Newman looked at her husband and repeated, "Your plan?"

He sighed. There was no point in continuing to pretend that he was sitting with her on the sofa because he was being threatened. He stood up.

"Helen, just be still," he said, and walked over to stand by Sutherland and look out the window.

"Butler!"

Butler and Luke Short turned at the sound of the voice, saw Sheriff Jim Courtwright approaching with two deputies in tow.

"What do you want, Courtwright?" Short asked.

"Shut your mouth, Luke," Courtwright said. "For a change I'm not lookin' for you this time." He pointed a finger at Butler. "I want him."

"What can I do for you, Sheriff?"

"You can give me your gun and come with me," Sheriff Courtwright said. "You're under arrest."

"For what?"

"Suspicion of murder."

"And who am I supposed to have murdered?"

"We'll talk about that in my office."

Courtwright reached for Butler's gun, but the gambler backed away.

"Don't make me use force, Butler."

"Sheriff," Butler said, "the man who killed Ed Cramer and the bartender, Zeke, is almost certainly in that house." He pointed.

"Al Newman's house?"

"That's right."

"What's he doing in there?"

"Waitin' for us," Short said.

"One man alone is waitin' to face the two of you?" he said, laughing. "That's rich. I've heard a lot of things about Sutherland, but I never heard that he had a death wish."

Butler and Short exchanged a glance.

"Who said anything about Sutherland?" Short asked.

"What?"

"We never mentioned Sutherland's name."

Courtwright looked confused, then trapped.

"Never mind that," he said. "Butler has to come with me."

"No," Butler said.

"You better go," Short said. "I can handle this. I'll come to the jail later with a lawyer."

"Luke, don't you see? This is what they want, to split us up. It's a plan." Butler looked at Courtwright. "A plan that's not going to work."

"Take him, boys," Courtwright said.

Butler and Short both drew their guns.

"Don't touch those guns," Butler said.

"Are you crazy?" Courtwright asked. "Drawing your guns on the law?"

"Right now we don't recognize your authority, Courtwright," Short said.

"Yeah," Butler said, "it's more than a little suspect, at the moment."

Courtwright turned and looked at his deputies.

"I said take him—take 'em both."

Both deputies gave him a look that said, "Why don't you take them yourself?"

"Goddamnit!" Courtwright said. "I'll have your badges."

The two deputies exchanged an anxious glance, then both unpinned their badges.

"You can have 'em," they said, handing their tin to the sheriff.

The two men walked away, leaving a confused Courtwright behind.

"Sheriff," Short said, "time to move along."

Courtwright turned a murderous gaze on Short.

"We're not through," he said. "I'll be back for you two with deputies I can trust."

"Make it a lot of them," Butler said.

Courtwright looked toward the house, then turned on his heels and stormed off.

"What the hell—" Sutherland said, inside the house. "What's goin' on?"

"Looks like Short and Butler stood them off," Newman said.

Sutherland dropped the curtain and looked at the lawyer.

"What now?"

Newman wasn't sure, and to cover up that fact he said, "Give me a minute."

Butler and Short watched Courtwright until he was out of sight, then holstered their guns and turned back to the house.

"We're going to have to pay for that," Butler said.

"We'll deal with it later," Short said. "Let's deal with this now. I think we've got him trapped in there."

"Back or front?' Butler asked.

"I'll take the front."

"Be careful."

"You too."

"Two minutes," Butler said, and then moved.

# CHAPTER 57

———◆———

When Butler reached the back, he tried the knob and found the door unlocked. He drew his gun, opened the door, and stepped in. He was in the kitchen and from there could hear Short's knock at the front door.

He crept through the kitchen and peered into the next room, the living room. It was empty. He entered and moved quickly to the front door. When he opened it he startled Luke Short.

"Jesus," Short said, "I almost shot you. What's goin' on?"

"I don't know," Butler said. "The house is empty."

"Somebody was in here," Short said. "They were watching us from that window. Let's check upstairs."

They did so, creeping up the stairs slowly. They found two bedrooms, both empty. They checked closets, and even looked under the beds. Convinced there was no one on the second level they came back down to the first, both baffled.

"Now what?" Butler asked.

"We couldn't have been wrong," Short said. "The

sheriff showin' up when he did tells me that. You were right, they were tryin' to split us up. Maybe we should've let them do it."

"You really think Sutherland would face you fairly, with no ace up his sleeve? Somebody probably would have back shot you from a window."

"Do you think Newman has chosen sides that clearly that he'd pick up a gun?" Short asked.

"I don't know what to think about him anymore," Butler admitted.

They both stood there, looking around them.

"There's got to be another way out of this house," Butler said finally. "Let's find it."

They split up and searched the house with their guns in their hands. They expected to find someone behind every door, but it wasn't until Butler tried a cupboard in the kitchen that he finally did.

"Luke?"

Short came running into the kitchen, found Butler in front of a walk-in cupboard. The shelves that held provisions stood open, having been built with hinges. It led to a staircase.

Butler pointed down.

"Root cellar?" Short asked.

"Only one way to find out."

Short peered down.

"It's dark."

"You got matches?"

"Yes."

"Let's find some candles."

They found some right on the shelves in front of

them. They each took one and lit it. With a candle in one hand, gun in the other, they went down.

It wasn't a cellar, but a tunnel that had been dug years ago. The wood shoring it up had started to collapse. There was dust on the floor, and three sets of footprints stood out starkly.

"I doubt anyone's used this tunnel for a long time before today," Short said.

They followed it until it ended at another staircase. The second step had recently broken beneath someone's weight.

"Let's hope the sonofabitch broke his leg," Butler said.

"Either one of them."

They went up the stairs, mindful of the fact that another step could also give way. They came to a door, opened it, and stepped into what appeared to be a storeroom.

"How far did we walk?" Short asked.

"A hundred yards or so."

They moved across the storeroom into the store proper. Empty shelves, a dusty counter. They were in a shop that had been closed up a long time.

"I don't get it," Short said. "Why take Mrs. Newman with them?"

"As a hostage?" Butler suggested. "Or to use as a shield?"

"Even I don't think Al Newman is that much of a sonofabitch," Short said.

"Maybe she's the brains," Butler said.

"Yeah, I'd believe that."

They had to force the front door to get outside. They found themselves on a block of stores right around the corner from the residential neighborhood where the Newman house was. When they turned and looked to see where they had come from, they saw a sign that read: NEWMAN'S HARDWARE.

"Newman's a lawyer. Was his father in hardware?" Butler asked.

"I don't know," Short said. "Does it matter? We've lost Sutherland, and Courtwright's going to be comin' for us with an army of deputies. Why don't you just mount up and ride out, Butler?"

"Save myself, you mean?"

"Yeah."

"Can't do that, Luke."

"Why the hell not? I would, if I wasn't knee-deep in the White Elephant."

"Sell out to Ward."

"I don't want to sell out," Short said. "I bought in for a reason."

"Well, I can't just ride out, so let's figure something out."

Short looked at his suit, which was now covered with dust from the tunnel.

"Let's get back," he said. "I want to wash up and change. I'd like to be clean when we face whatever's coming."

# CHAPTER 58

They went back to the White Elephant, had baths, changed their clothes, and met in the dining room. Short had decided he not only wanted to face what was coming while clean, but also with a steak in his belly. They both ordered a sirloin with all the trimmings. That was when Bill Ward found them.

"I've been looking all over for you two," Ward said, seating himself at their table. "Tell me what's going on with Al Newman?"

"Do you really want to know" Short asked.

"I asked, didn't I?"

Short looked at Butler who shrugged, giving him the floor. Short told Ward everything they knew, and everything they thought they knew.

"Jesus," Ward said, "are you sure about all of this?"

"No doubt."

"Well, I know Newman's father did have a hardware store," Ward said.

"Great," Butler said, "now tell us why he'd get mixed up with someone like Sutherland, and why he'd drag his own wife into it?"

"I don't know," Ward said, frowning. "The sheriff was here looking for you two. He had half a dozen deputies with him. I'm getting the feeling you should turn yourselves in. Luke, let him lay out his evidence against you in a court of law."

"Courtwright will make sure Luke never gets to court," Butler said.

"He just wants to run you out of town, Butler," Ward said. "Why not let him do it?"

"I'll let him do it, all right," Butler said, "as soon as we finish with Sutherland and Newman."

"Well . . ."

"Bill, do you know something?" Short asked.

"Nothing definite," Ward said, "but if Al Newman has kept his father's shop closed up all these years, he might have also kept his father's house."

"And you know just where that is, don't you?" Butler asked.

Ward looked at both of them and nodded.

"This is some big old house," Sutherland said. "Why keep it boarded up? Why not live in it instead of that smaller one you're in?"

"It was my father's," Newman said. "Not mine to live in."

"Albert," Helen Newman said, "I insist you make this man go away."

"Ma'am," Sutherland asked, "just what is it you don't like about me?"

"I don't like the way you act, the way you look," she said, "and I most assuredly do not like the way you smell."

"Yeah," Sutherland said, with a laugh, "but other than that?"

"Sutherland, I think my wife is right," Newman said. "I think perhaps you should stay the night here, and then be on your way."

"On my way where?"

"Well . . . leave town."

"Why would I leave Fort Worth?" Sutherland asked. "I like it here."

"Well, the law . . ."

"The law's not lookin' for me," Sutherland said. "They're lookin' for Luke Short, and for Butler."

"Then why not let the law have them?"

"Because I want them," Sutherland said. "Those two have been up my ass for too long. It's because of them I had to kill Cramer and Zeke. It's because of them the Bloody Spur is boarded up."

"You . . . are a murderer?" Helen Newman said, shocked.

"Aw, Ma'am," Sutherland asked, "what did you think I was?"

# CHAPTER 59

―――――●◆●――――

"Here we are again," Short said.

They were outside the house on Pennsylvania Avenue where Al Newman's father had lived and, presumably, Newman himself had grown up.

"They've got to be inside," Butler said. "Sutherland's got no place else to go."

"He can go home," Luke Short pointed out. "The law's not lookin' for him, they're lookin' for us."

"Okay," Butler said. "Let's knock, this time. They're not expecting us."

"Fine," Short said, "we'll walk right up to the front door and knock."

When the knock came at the door, Sutherland looked to Newman.

"Who knows we're here?"

"No one."

"You sent for the law before, for Short and Butler," Sutherland said. "How do I know that ain't the law at the door for me?"

"Like you said," Newman pointed out, "the law isn't looking for you."

Sutherland moved to Helen Newman's side, grabbed her arm and pulled his gun.

"Hey, there's no need—"

"Find out who it is," he said to the lawyer, "and get rid of them."

When Newman opened the door and saw Butler and Short standing there he said, "He's inside. He has a gun on Helen."

"Tell him to come out," Short said. "Tell him we'll do it, just him and me. After all, that's what he wants."

"Luke—" Butler started.

"Just tell him, Newman."

Newman went back into the house, leaving the door open.

"Should we go in?" Butler asked.

"Let's wait," Short said. "Let's just give him what he wants and get this over with."

When Newman reappeared in the doorway, Sutherland was behind him, still holding Helen.

"Sonofabitch," he said. "It is you."

"Come on, Sutherland," Short said. "Let's get this over with so I can get back to my life."

"What about you?" the man asked Butler. "You just gonna watch?"

"Yep," Butler said, "and if you kill Luke, you'll have your try at me."

Sutherland frowned.

"How do I know this is on the up and up?" he asked. "What if I step out there and you both gun me?"

"You have my word," Short said.

"And you?" Sutherland asked Butler.

"My word, too," Butler said. "We just want to end this."

"So do I," Sutherland said. "I can't find anybody good enough to send after you two, so I might as well just do it myself."

Butler looked at Newman.

"You got a gun on you?"

"No."

"In the house?"

"No."

"If you come up with a gun," Butler said, "I'll kill you."

"I have no gun."

"Okay, then," Short said, "can we get this under way?

"Back up, both of you," Sutherland said. "Down the stairs. Butler, you stand off to the right where I can see you."

Butler and Short did as they were told. Butler moved off to the right, wondering if they should have gotten his word that he wouldn't try to kill them while standing behind Newman's wife.

"Counselor," Sutherland said, "here. You take your wife."

He pushed Helen Newman toward her husband, who caught her.

"As my lawyer, am I in any trouble after I kill these two?"

"Not with us as witnesses that it was a fair fight both times."

"I won't say—" Helen Newman started.

"Shut up, Helen!" Newman snapped.

"That ain't no way to talk to your wife, Al," Sutherland said, and stepped down off the porch.

# CHAPTER 60

Sutherland holstered his gun, pointed at Butler.

"Now you stand your ground, gambler."

"I'm waiting my turn, Sutherland," Butler said, "but don't think I'll be getting it."

"You got that much confidence in your friend, here?" Sutherland asked.

"You know Luke Short's reputation," Butler said. "What do you think?"

"You're a gamblin' man," Sutherland said. "How much money you got in your wallet right now?"

"A couple of thousand."

"That much?" Sutherland was impressed.

"Like you said, I'm a gambler."

"You willin' to put that much money on your friend?" Sutherland asked. "I'll match it. If I kill 'im, you pay me before we face off."

"I'm right here," Luke Short said. "Don't talk about me like I'm not right here."

"That's a bet."

"You heard him, Counselor," Sutherland said. "We got a bet."

"I heard him."

"Let's do it, Short."

"They're betting their lives?" Helen said to her husband.

"They're gamblers, Helen."

"And this is what you aspire to, Albert?"

"All my life," he said. "My father would never let me."

"And I held you back, too?"

"Yes."

"I suppose I don't really know you at all, do I?"

"No," Newman said. "I suppose not."

Butler had the urge to simply draw and fire, killing Sutherland where he stood. Why play it fair? He'd already tried to ambush, or have them ambushed, several times. Why should they play fair with him?

What if he really was good enough to kill Luke Short?

Short pushed back the flap of his coat, transferred his cane to his left hand.

"For such a little man," Sutherland said to the diminutive gambler, "killin' you is sure gonna make me a big one."

"You might kill me, Sutherland," Short said, "but you're never going to be a big man."

"I guess we'll see."

"Not if you don't stop talkin'."

Sutherland laughed and went for his gun . . .

To Butler it happened within a split second. Sutherland's move was like lightning, and yet by the time he had his gun in his hand, Luke Short had already shot him once. He added a second bullet for good measure. Both shots hit Sutherland in the chest, around his heart, and could have been covered by a palm.

Butler walked to where Short was standing over the man's body. Short kicked the man's gun away, replaced his spent shells with live ones, and holstered his own weapon.

"He had a helluva move," he said.

"Yep," Butler said.

"You know," Luke Short said, "after all we've been through, it wasn't much of an ending."

"At least it's over, though."

"We'll have to explain it to the law."

"We have witnesses," Butler said.

"Do you think Newman will back us?"

While Luke Short and Butler watched, Al Newman turned to his wife, guided her inside, and closed the door behind them.

"I think she will," Butler said.

"And what about him?" Short asked. "What happens to him?"

"I'm still not sure what his part in all of this was," Butler said, "but like you said, he won't be playing in any of your games anymore."

"Nope."

Short used his cane to nudge Sutherland's body just once, then looked at Butler.

"Guess you'll be leavin'."

"As soon as we get the loose ends cleared up, get you straight with the law."

"Hey, that bet you made on me? The two thousand?"

"Yeah?"

"You ain't never gonna collect."

Butler laughed.

"I knew that when I made the bet."